THE STATE OF
MONTANA

MAXIM JAKUBOWSKI

Maxim Jakubowski was born in the UK but brought up in Paris. He followed a career in publishing by opening the Murder One bookshop in London. He writes, edits, and publishes in many areas of genre fiction, including science fiction and fantasy, mystery, and erotica. He is the editor of the bestselling *Mammoth Book of Erotica* series, which has now reached 12 volumes, including two acclaimed books of erotic photography. As a publisher he has been responsible for various cult imprints including Black Box Thrillers, Blue Murder, and Eros Plus, and he currently runs the provocative Neon list. He has published over 50 books of his own, including *Life in the World of Women, The State of Montana, Kiss Me Sadly, Confessions of a Romantic Pornographer*, and the *Skin in Darkness* trilogy, which collects *It's You that I Want to Kiss, Because She Thought She Loved Me,* and *On Tenderness Express.* Blue Moon will soon be publishing a new collection of his erotic short stories *Fools for Lust*, alongside the Thunder's Mouth publication of *American Casanova*, the first ever "round-robin" erotic novel, which he has conceived and directed.

He is the Literary Director of London's *Crime Scene* film festival, a columnist for the *Guardian*, feature writer for *The Times*, and a regular broadcaster and television commentator in the UK and Europe. He is also a past winner of the Anthony Award.

His next novel will be *I Was Waiting for You*.

THE STATE OF MONTANA

MONTANA

A NOVELLA OF EROTICA

MAXIM JAKUBOWSKI

BLUE MOON BOOKS
NEW YORK

The State of Montana
Copyright © 1998, 2006 by Maxim Jakubowski

Published by
Blue Moon Books
An Imprint of Avalon Publishing Group Incorporated
245 West 17th Street, 11th floor
New York, NY 10011-5300

First Blue Moon Books Edition 2006

First Published in 1998 by The Do-Not Press

ISBN: 1-56201-489-7
ISBN-13: 978-1-56201-489-6

9 8 7 6 5 4 3 2 1

Printed in Canada
Distributed by Publishers Group West

THE STATE OF
MONTANA

The Indifference of Heaven

Montana had never been to Montana.

Or even anywhere close.

Her friend Stephanie had warned her never to use her real name when talking to strangers on the chat lines.

"I call myself Ghostlight," Stephanie revealed. "It's exotic, unusual, catches people's attention. Not at all like my own name..."

Montana's real name was Adrienne. She'd never liked it anyway.

She ransacked her memory for a name, a word that would suit her and finally reached back to her childhood when, for weeks on end, she had inhabited an imaginary world in her mind where she was none other than an audacious cowgirl roaming the plains, between open skies and chilly valleys, wielding a mighty whip and a shotgun. There had been an old black and white western movie on television, which the family had all watched in their previous Longuieul apartment, with Barbara Stanwyck—or was it Jane Wyman?—as the indomitable heroine, and it had somehow caught Adrienne's fertile imagination in a big way. Memories of it were still vague today, and she was now unsure whether the TV Montana had actually been a good gal or a baddie. But the name had stuck.

Her new Internet persona would be Montana.

So, tonight, as she tossed and turned in the marital bed in the Montreal night, craving sleep to fill the emptiness, her dreams kept on returning to the unending plains and the big blue sky of the faraway American state, to distant hills capped with snow and posses of wild horses racing through the wilderness.

The bedroom was quiet. The sound of cars racing down the

nearby highway to Ontario was muted and the familiar rhythm of her sleeping husband's snores no longer bothered her in the slightest. She had had almost seven years to get accustomed to it.

The snores took a respite. She looked round at her sleeping husband, almost as if she were still unused to the sight of this large, inert body sharing the geography of the bed with her. On the bedside table on her side, the baby alarm's small red light winked continuously. The child was now past three, but out of habit they had not yet disconnected the apparatus connecting them to the crib down the corridor.

It was a girl. Vanessa, he had wanted to call her. So they did. Adrienne would have preferred to name her Mireille, after her grandmother. But Vanessa it had been. It wasn't that his will had turned out to be stronger than hers. More the effect of surprise at finding herself so suddenly a mother, like a shock to the system at being confronted with this minuscule, living thing they had consciously made together. The pregnancy seemed to have gone so fast. So, come the naming of the baby, still reeling with genuine surprise, she had given in on Vanessa. She no longer had the energy to argue, negotiate, compromise.

The baby had arrived so quickly. Of course, in her mind and from her distended appearance, she had known that the nine months were almost up. But the circumstances had proven unexpected. She had gotten a strong stomachache after too heavy a meal at her in-laws and took a precautionary trip to the hospital, during which time the two of them had replayed the mathematics of the pregnancy over and over again, only to jointly agree it was still a couple of weeks early.

The pain had increased while they were still in the brightly lit waiting room.

"Ouch!" she had complained.

"Is it getting worse?" her husband had asked.

"It's not the baby," she had said with an air of certitude, holding her breath back. "I really have to go to the toilet."

"Are you sure?"

"Of course," she had shouted at him, "do you think I don't know when I have to take a shit?"

Of course, she had been wrong and it had been their daughter about to make her first appearance on the scene. Taking a shit or delivering a baby, it had initially felt much the same to her in the muddle of her pain and acute constipation.

It was a moment her husband had never allowed her to forget, and which no doubt Vanessa would learn about when old enough, the sorry story of how her mother had once confused her with faecal matter.

As Adrienne's husband groaned in his sleep, her thoughts drifted back to the here and now. This man, her husband. A good man, the father of their child. Yes, he loved her; she knew that. And she loved him back—or, at any rate, she thought she did. It was just that sometimes this thing called love seemed to elude her. There was a man—was it already ten years ago?— who had told her in anger that she had a cold heart. She had then indifferently acknowledged the fact. If such was the case, she accepted it gladly. It seldom bothered her. After all, other people were sometimes so unnecessarily emotional. Not her problem.

Still floating in layers of sleep, her husband's bulk shifted. His body moved nearer to hers between the crisp white sheets, unconsciously seeking her heat.

This morning—was it three or four in the morning? she couldn't see the reading on the clock alarm from her position in the bed—she didn't pull back from his contact. She had been awake for so long now that his warmth was welcome.

He cradled himself against the small of her back, adjusting his stance to fit her shape.

The bump of his penis was already hardening as it grazed her skin.

Adrienne extended her arm down to her husband's crotch, making a way through the tangled covers. Yes, he was already half-erect. Her fingers tightened gently around the base of his awakening cock, taking the silent pulse of his dormant desire.

"Do you want to?" she asked him.

Outside the window the distant stars were already making way for early morning banks of low clouds that were moving in from the south.

"Hmmm . . ." he mumbled, shifting again so that his cock uncoiled to full, aroused length, away from the rampart of her body. She still held it between three fingers, feeling its slow, steady growth to hardness. She finally let go, a lone finger straying over its tip, where the glans peeked through the shrivelled foreskin, smooth, almost damp to her touch.

"That's nice," he remarked, his voice moving from slumber to wakefulness. His whole body straightened, spread-eagled itself between sheet and bedcover, toes stretching at an acute angle towards the foot of their bed. His customary pose of prone sexual acceptance.

Adrienne repositioned herself on her side, now facing the extended shape of her husband and pulled the cover back to unveil his body in the semidarkness of their bedroom.

She distractedly kept on stroking his jutting cock as he opened his eyes and silently beckoned her to maybe take him into her mouth. She remained silent as the invisible dialogue of married-life sex quietly moved between them, swirling between the heat their now partly uncovered bodies were generating. His left arm rose towards her and his hand cupped her right breast, fingering the nipple into a hard, elongated ball of pliant, darker flesh. Still, her mouth kept safely away from his cock. Now, she closed her eyes in turn—imagining the first time the hands of a man had touched her breasts—and attempted to recapture that indefinable feeling, that nervous prelude to the electricity of pleasure. Between her fingers, his cock twitched.

Already?

How come men could wake already hard and ready for it?

Did he dream of her, of other girls, of sex, even in his sleep? How much she would have liked to read his dreams of lust.

"Now?" she asked him.

Her husband nodded.

She twisted round and straddled him as he opened his legs wider to welcome her onto his lap. Still stroking him, humouring his hardness, Adrienne used her other hand to open her lips wider, she was barely wet, just a bit sticky. She brought her fingers to her lips and dribbled some saliva onto them which she used to lubricate herself more and then impaled herself on him.

He held his breath as his cock dug into her, submerged by her warmth.

Right then, their daughter coughed, back in her room and the sound echoed loudly through the plastic speaker of the baby alarm standing on the flimsy wicker table near them. Their movements stopped suddenly as they both listened for more. But there were no more noises from the child and, mind again at rest, her husband began thrusting into her with staccato movements, pushing himself higher into her, then partly out again and in and out and in and out. Each of his movements stretched her outer lips farther and farther apart as his lovemaking sought to bury his shaft deeper and deeper inside her vagina, the tip of his fully extended cock sometimes brushing against her inner walls as his motion became more metronomic. His eyes were closed. Both his arms were extended forward, towards her torso, mechanically kneading her breasts.

The glimmer of pleasure at last began inside her. A pleasant tingle in the hollow of her stomach, like a small electric shock extending ever so slowly onwards from that uncharted inner territory surrounding her cunt, onward to her darkening nipples, reverberating all the way up to her brain.

Then, all too quickly, her husband convulsed and groaned and Adrienne felt his come spurt inside her, bathing her innards with its perfunctory warmth. The glimmer inside her faded fast as his thrusts settled down and, flat on his back, under her, he expelled most of the air that had been stored in his lungs while they fucked to indicate his pleasure had come, and gone. For another half minute or so, she took over the movement and rocked herself up and down on his shaft, in a vain attempt to recover the needed contact between cock and sensitive inside walls. But she soon lost touch with the evanescent feeling as he detumesced and she felt his ejaculate begin to seep out of her through the growing gap between their linked genitals and dribble onto her open thighs.

She disengaged from him, now dripping onto the sheets; he rolled sideways and took a box of Kleenex from his side of the bed and handed one to her. As she used it to dam the gooey flow, he used another to wipe his penis clean, an old automatic habit of his she had always hated. As if he were wiping himself clean of her, so quickly after the act. Ashamed of her inner juices, her smell.

He straightened up in the bed and threw the soiled tissue into the bin.

"That was nice, Adie," he said. "It's been a long time since we'd done it in the morning."

She didn't answer.

Outside the window, the morning sky paraded its customary shade of grey.

❐

This was Monday, her day off work.

After Vanessa's birth, they had taken a hard look at their financial situation and jointly came to the conclusion that with the regular interest generated by a recent inheritance from his grandfather, together with his earnings at the computer consultancy, it was no longer necessary for Adrienne to work at the bank. The human resources people at Citicorp had suggested she not make an immediate decision about this, just in case she later changed her mind. They knew her well and, six months after the baby's birth, she decided to return to her position there as an investment analyst. Sitting at home all day to look after the child had grown boring and frustrating. Vanessa was a quiet, happy, but withdrawn child, who actually didn't need that much close care. And with Adrienne's salary boosting their joint income, they could easily afford a daily childminder.

The one compromise she agreed to with her husband was to restrict herself to a four-day week at the bank and take Mondays off. They both had a computer at home, so work could always be done there if the need arose. But it seldom did.

Breakfast had come and gone in silence. Her husband was gone for the day and Vanessa had been bathed and fed by Natalie the childminder, before being dropped off at the local play school. Natalie would return there at twelve to pick her up.

Adrienne placed the bowls, plates, and glasses in the dishwasher and, clad only in her usual fluffy white bathrobe, walked into the study. She knew she should take a shower but a glance at the digital wall clock indicated that it was the beginning of the afternoon in Europe.

She had often dreamed of Europe years back, but had never been there. She and Pierre had become engaged whilst studying at the local university, and once they had both graduated and started working, they had sensibly foregone luxuries like holidays in order to save for the deposit on their first piece of property together. It seemed the right thing to do at the time. They had married as soon as they'd had enough in their joint bank account for the down payment. It had been a nice two bedroom apartment on the French hill. But, out of habit, they had kept on saving assiduously thereafter, and within two years had upgraded to their current house in the suburbs. It had all seemed so easy. The engagement, the marriage, the apartment, the house, the baby. So organized and predictable. Now, Adrienne sort of wondered where all the time had gone, how she had never seemed to have the time to even think about things, about life. A honeymoon in Jamaica, where he'd caught a stomach bug. Occasional holidays in Florida. Biannual trips to Ontario for family outings. Routine had taken over so quickly.

In a few months, she would be thirty-two. Not a major birthday, she knew. But a strange age to be. If you'd never even been to Europe.

Her cunt felt clammy, but the laptop lay open on the desk in the study. The shower would have to wait. She switched on the computer, an old Compaq, and watched the blue screen appear as the computer booted up. She waited impatiently. It was so much slower than the desk computer she used at the office.

With a few keystrokes on the sleek keyboard, she logged on to the Internet and connected with the chat line.

She was no longer Adrienne in Montreal. She was now Montana.

She glanced quickly at the long list of names, the "handles" on display in the rectangular box in the top right quadrant of the screen. Many were familiar to her, even without her recourse to the "Friends" tab, some were new.

The names, the pseudonyms, the subtle and the unclever, the liars, the indifferent and the desperate: *9 inches & thick. A. Amour. Aromafem. Attika (FR). Bayou. Bel Ria. Bettie Page. Big One for You. Bi f London for bi f. Bi m free massage NY. Bob. Bobbie (Sw). Bored wife for fone sex. Boy 19. Busty Babe. California guy's little slut. Cantata. Carl. Chris (m). Christine. CK. Clare (loves anal). Corrina. Cple for bi f. Courtney. Cree (Oz). DeeDee. Des (f). Dominique for f only. DJ. Doctor. Dreams. Dunc (scot). Dungeon denizen. Early and lonely. Elmer. Elusive. f for f (busy). Enormous black cock. For older women. Fred. Grace. Haircutter. Hard for you. Helen. Hermann. HiMaintenance. Holly. Horny. Hot and Hungry. Hugh Jarse. Hunter. Ian. Italian guy. Irving. Janwillem. Jen. Jerry. Jonny. Juliete. Juergen. Impaler (Philly). Kate. Kit Kat. Kristin. Lolita. Lonely. Louise. Lucy. MadLove. Marcelo Masturbani. married m for affair. m for cple. M for married f. Marc. Master. maxine. Mercy. Miaw McKenna. mk. Montana. Mr & Mrs UK. Naked in office. Nathalie.*

Nate. Naughty girl. On the beach. Orgy boy. Paul. Penetrator. pete. Peter. Photographer. Quality fem wanted. Rachel (for pictures). rachel. Really big. Really nice guy. Rob & Dee. Ruth. Sarah Bond. Scott in ny. Seattle. Seek f for harem. Sensuous sculptress. Soleil. Stella for f. Steff. Stephanie. Sub f. The original nice guy. Tim S. Tom Cruise lookalike. US gal in Switzerland. Teacher for v. yng. girl. Voodoo. Well-endowed. Wet and willing. Wife away. Younger sister.

He was there.

Montana moved her mouse over to the *mk* line, just an inch or so away from her own nickname on the ever-changing list and clicked on "Talk."

Montana: Hello, my love. Am I disturbing you? Talking to anyone else?

mk: Hi. No, I was just hanging around here waiting for you, watching the cyber-landscape.

Montana: You don't have to say that to please me, u know. I don't mind if you talk to others …

mk: It's OK. I only came online a few minutes before you. It's Monday, our time to talk. How could I ever forget?

Montana: You're sweet-talking me again!

mk: As ever …

Montana: So how's your week been, my love?

mk: Much the same as usual. Days just drifted by and away. Thought of you a lot.

Montana: So did I.

mk: You always say that, Montana.

Montana: Well, I do. You're very special to me. Like a ray of sunshine in my drab life, you know.

mk: But not enough to agree to see me, hey?

Montana: There you go again, Martin. You never give up, do you?

mk: The day I give up on you, Montana, is the day I give up on living …

Montana: You naughty man, is that a threat, emotional blackmail?

mk: No. Just a statement of fact.

Montana: Are you going to make me sad again today, because if that's what you intend to do, I'd rather go! I'm not in the mood for contrariness right now.

mk: OK, I'll be good. Behave. So, on your own, childminder and daughter away? Just you and me on the screen? What are you wearing?

Montana: Just my bathrobe. I was going to take my shower and realised you might be online already. The clocks changed, moved back one hour last week. Wasn't sure whether I'd missed you because of the new time difference.

mk: They also changed here. Anything underneath that bathrobe?

Montana: No. Slipped it on as I got out of bed.

mk: Oh, Montana, just the thought of you nude under that flimsy piece of cloth is enough to make me crazy. I want you so much ...

Montana: I like it when you say things like that. I do.

mk: You'd like it even more if I were there in the flesh to say all those things, and so much more. In person.

Montana: I know I would, Martin, but I can't allow that. Isn't it enough for you to know that I love you deeply, that there's a very special place for you right there inside my heart?

mk: Here we go again ... It's not what I call love, and you know that, Montana. Love is more. Not just a whim, it's more than feelings or emotions, you see, it requires bodies to meet, embrace. I can't survive on this second division version of love. I require reality.

Montana: You need the physical side, I know. But I'm married, I love my child and husband and cannot take the risk of losing them, Martin. I can't allow it to go that far. And even if I did, what would happen after? Would I be any happier knowing it's happened and that the reality you invoke prevents us both from going any further down that road. I'd feel betrayed, used ...

mk: How you make me suffer, Montana ... you know it would only take a word from you and I would be on the first plane to Canada. Please think hard about it, do change your mind. All I'm asking for is a drink in a cafe, a meal, to be able to talk to you. Does the idea of actually meeting me scare you so much?

Montana: Yes, Martin. Because if we did meet, we both know it might happen and I cannot take that risk. We've talked about this so many times before …

mk: I know. But will not give up on you.

Montana: You lovely man. I still love you very much, u know.

mk: Enough, my sweet Montana, you're just going to make me sadder and angrier.

Montana: But I don't want to make you sad. If that is the case today, maybe I should log off?

mk: No. STAY.

Montana: OK.

mk: When you take that shower later, think of me invisibly present between the droplets of water pearling down your body while you soap your breasts.

Montana: mmmmmmm …

mk: Imagine how my fingers would clean you slowly, moving from the valley of your cleavage down and further down towards your sweet intimacy …

Montana: mmmmmmmm … I love it when you talk to me like that. No other man ever has.

mk: None of your other Internet lovers? Really?

Montana: You know that I have no other lovers here, just friends. All we do is chat harmlessly. Martin, you are the only man I have sent my photo to.

mk: And I fell in love with that photo, Montana. But I beg you to send me another. I want to see your eyes. A photograph without those damn sunglasses. I want to see more of your face, you bewitching woman.

Montana: I promise I'll look for one. I'm the one who takes the snaps in the family so there aren't many of me around. But I'll search for a suitable picture and try and scan it.

mk: An unsuitable one would do ...

Montana: I don't have any either. Well, some years back my husband took a photograph of my chest. In black and white, you can't even see my face. Like a piece of meat. I don't like that picture at all.

mk: My mouth is watering already, my sweet love.

Montana: Don't hold your breath.

mk: So, Montana, where now?

Montana: What do you mean?

mk: I'm not even sure myself. I seem to be running out of words, of arguments, reasons to convince you, to seduce you ... What is it now? Eight months we've been talking here almost daily and I don't think I have much energy to continue fighting like this ...

Montana: But we're not fighting!

mk: I am, an uphill struggle to gain access to your distant heart.

Montana: But you are already in my heart, deep deep inside. Believe me. And when the day is grey like today, you feel like a ray of sunshine. You light up my life. Always remember that.

mk: It just doesn't feel that way. I love you. I want you. Badly.

Montana: Martin, you have me.

mk: Have I really?

Montana: Yes.

Their chat line conversations invariably led to the same dead end these days. Going round and round. Declarations, assurances, sarcasm, fervour, sadness and anger, a waltz of words on flickering screens, with increasing periods of silence between the lines when one or the other ran out of words to say.

Montana: Are you still there?

mk: Yes.

Montana: Busy elsewhere?

mk: No. Just thinking.

Montana: Of what?

mk: Of the color of your nipples.

Montana: You make me smile, you know.

mk: My pleasure entirely.

Montana: Is that irony or bitterness?

mk: Both.

Montana: Anyway, I have to go take that shower now. I have my salsa class in a couple of hours downtown.

mk: I'd love to see you dance.

Montana: Close your eyes and imagine it. You're so good at imagining things, Martin. I'd love if you could send me another e-mail like you did in December. About the two of us, on that tropical beach, sunning ourselves in the nude, with all the colours of the sea and sand surrounding us. You never did finish that story, did you?

mk: I need more inspiration!

Montana: You're just being naughty, now . . . Please, I like it so much when you tell me stories about the two of us.

mk: But will there ever be two of us?

Montana: We're already together, Martin. We always will be, in my mind. Look, I have to go, really. Or I'll be late for the class.

mk: Enjoy your dancing, then. I'll be thinking of you.

Montana: I know. And it would nice to get an e-mail.

mk: Maybe.

Montana: Bye my love.

mk: cya.

Montana: xxxxxxxxxxx

mk: x

Montana drove towards the airport, her wicker basket on the passenger seat beside her. It was filled with her billowing salsa dress and black bolero top, still in the dry cleaner's plastic wrap. The traffic on the highway was light for the time of day. As she drove parallel to the airport's perimeter barbed-wire fence, she watched a Northwest jumbo land and an American Airlines cargo flight take off in a flurry of dust.

A road sign indicated the major junction ahead where the whirlpool of highways merged and bifurcated in all directions. One wrong turn (or a right one?) and a couple of days later she would find herself in Calgary or Vancouver. Two more places she had never visited. Cruising the sargasso of airport hotels was the nearest Montana had ever come to exotic travel.

Today, she selected the Stouffer Madison. The hotels with underground car parking facilities were preferable. More unlikely for anyone she knew to spot her three-year-old white Lexus, a present from her husband when she had become pregnant. Not that anybody she might know ever came around here in the daytime, whether friends, bank clients, acquaintances.

She manoeuvred the car into a corner spot on the first lower level, locked her wicker basket into the boot and took a lift to the hotel lobby. She was wearing one of her office power suits, a two-piece grey striped tailleur with a low hemline that reached just above her knees. And opaque stockings. Montana knew her legs were her best asset. Long, rangy without being thin. And this was the best way to display them. Black low-heeled leather shoes complemented the ensemble, highlighting the sleek, pale curve of her calves.

There were few people in the bar area. Just one barman in attendance, polishing the liquor glasses, and a maid dusting the the glass-topped tables, lost in daydreams of escape. Montana found a seat, halfway between the entrance to the low-ceilinged, half-lit room and the bar counter, where she could strategically survey the whole area.

She wasn't noticed for a couple of minutes.

Finally, the barman walked over and she ordered her drink, a vodka with orange. Looked around her. A couple in the opposite corner, sipping tea or coffee, probably checked out and still too early to make their way to the airport to catch their flight home. Stray businessmen looking bored, nursing half-empty glasses. She often wondered about the people who briefly inhabited airport hotels, what they did, why they were here, how come they had so much time on their hands? She felt safe in temporary places such as this.

She cupped her glass in both hands, sunk deeper into the softness of the plush chair, watched the two cubes of ice slowly melt inside her glass. The lipstick trace of her lips adhered to the edge of the glass. Adrienne never wore lipstick at the bank, at home or socially, only at the hotels. Montana sighed deeply and briefly closed her eyes.

Which is when the suit walked in to the hotel bar.

With his carefully groomed slicked-back greying hair, charcoal black loafer shoes and sky blue button down collar shirt, he looked around the room and took note of her, the only woman in the place, before he moved on to the bar and lowered himself on to a high stool at the end of the crescent-shaped counter.

She heard him order a Jack Daniels on the rocks. He carried neither briefcase nor attache case with him.

Montana silently sipped her drink, occasionally attempting to recognize a particular song here and there amongst the blur of the Muzak that piped out quietly from the bar's hidden speakers.

On several occasions, when she looked up, she noticed the man glancing at her with increased curiosity. Lunchtime neared and the room began to fill. There were other single men around now, but most of them appeared to have a private agenda, either drinking too fast, making every minute of alcohol consumption count or checking their watches at regular intervals, waiting for someone to join them.

Montana gave the suit a final once-over and reflected he would do. Neither too young nor too old, suitably dressed, seemingly fit, good-looking, too, in a bland sort of conformist way.

The next time he glanced in her direction, she flashed him a gentle smile of recognition.

He smiled back, a tad surprised by her acknowledgment.

Minutes later, as she knew and hoped he would, he asked if

he could join her. She agreed. He brought his drink over from the bar and settled into the armchair facing her.

"Another drink?"

"Sure. That would be nice."

He hailed the bartender. Stuck to mineral water for himself.

"Are you waiting for anyone?" he asked her.

"No." She did not elaborate.

"I'm staying at the hotel," he informed her. "A day to kill at the fag end of a business trip. The symposium I was attending ended a day earlier than I thought."

The drinks he had ordered arrived. Montana emptied what remained of her first vodka and orange into the new glass, filling it to the brim. She was a slow drinker. She did not respond to the information he had volunteered. The suit persevered.

"I'm from Detroit. My name's Anthony. Tony, if you prefer."

"Mine is Belle de Jour," she replied.

He was silent for a moment, digesting her words.

"That's certainly unusual," he answered. "Rings a bell somehow." He laughed quietly, suddenly realising his involuntary pun.

He looked Montana in the eyes quite solemnly and asked, "It would feel odd calling you Belle. I accept your discretion and the use of an alias but, won't you tell me your real name? Please?" he pleaded.

She steadily held his gaze.

"Montana. My name is Montana," she revealed.

The man smiled broadly.

"That's also pretty unusual, but it'll do."

She smiled back at him.

In turn, he looked the carefully groomed young blonde woman up and down. She certainly was a striking specimen, he thought. The jacket of her suit was partly unbuttoned and unveiled the outset of her cleavage. She didn't appear very opulent but he did wonder whether she was wearing a brassiere underneath. Something told him she wasn't. She crossed her long legs and he heard the unmistakable ruffle of nylon against nylon and skin. Her eyes were pale green, her lips thin but bright red. She didn't appear to be wearing any other make-up. She continued to smile back at him, enigmatically, indulgently.

A host of contradictory thoughts and questions swirled across the man's mind. A woman in a hotel bar, attractive, with a touch of class but not really the type, surely?

"I'm available," she said softly.

"You mean . . . ?" his glass froze in motion between the table and his mouth, as her sudden statement took him by surprise.

"I mean I'm yours if you want me."

He set his glass down without taking a further sip of water.

"You said you had a room upstairs?" she asked.

Maybe she should have accepted his civilized offer to have a bite to eat first, but now they were in his hotel room.

The man suggested she help herself to anything from the minibar while he quickly tidied away the clothes and thick files that sprawled across the bed, but Montana declined. She stood there watching him, reflecting on the anonymity of all hotel rooms and the curious universal smell that emanated from them. She couldn't put a finger on it. But it was the same, whether luxury inns or cheap motels, it was always the same. Maybe it was the smell of sex, she reckoned. The fragrance bequeathed by the hundreds of couples who had fucked in this small enclosure, the solitary men and women who had masturbated wildly in the privacy of the room to personal memories of times past, daydreams of partners who would never be or to the Technicolor images of tawdry magazines or the pay-per-view erotic channel on the television set in the corner.

On a desk next to the TV set lay a laptop computer, a model she wasn't familiar with.

Montana wondered what Martin, her virtual London lover, was doing now. Probably about to leave his office, she guessed.

She knew he always worked late. He was also a man who travelled much and spent many hours in hotels. Had he ever been in this room? Touched a woman here, stroked his cock with thoughts of her?

"There we are." The man had completed his tidying up. "Everything's presentable now."

"I'll pass on the drink," Montana said, facing him. She had dropped her small handbag to the floor.

"So?" the man said.

"So," Montana replied.

"I must say I wasn't expecting this encounter at all," he said. "Not quite sure how to begin," he added.

Montana looked him in the eyes. In the plainly lit room, he now looked like the tired mid-forties businessman he really was. In the bar, there had been something more dashing about him. But she was here, she had committed to her decision and was ready to go through with it.

"I'll do anything you want me to . . ."

"Oh . . ."

"And you can do anything you want with me. But there's one thing, though . . ."

"Yes?"

"I won't kiss."

"I see."

The man now seemed strangely hesitant.

"You're married, aren't you?" she inquired.

"Yes, I am."

"Does she still give you head?"

"No. Not really, not often," he confessed.

Montana moved towards him and helped him slip his jacket off. He carefully draped it over the back of a chair.

"Sit down on the edge of the bed," she urged him.

He did.

As he sat, the bulge of his middle-aged stomach pressed against the alignment of the buttons on his blue shirt and disturbed their impeccable alignment, while straining against the belt circling the top of his trousers. Montana's hands moved closer. She loosened the metallic buckle and undid the brown leather belt. She fumbled momentarily for a hold on the zip, then pulled on it and opened up her access to the man's lower stomach.

He was wearing grey boxer shorts, cinched tight at his waist. She slipped her hand below the elastic and felt his warm cock, nesting in a forest of rough curls. Even though he was still soft, he felt big.

But also different to the touch.

"Raise your ass one moment," she ordered him.

He obeyed and she pulled the boxer shorts down altogether. His cock spilled out as Montana watched. He was circumcised. Few of her men had been before. The spectacle of the purple mushroom leaping quite pink and naked from the stem of his thick penis without the assistance of an erection was an unusual sight for her.

It looked so raw.

She lowered her face towards him and examined the rough lines where, decades ago no doubt, the foreskin had been cut away. You could still see the scar. Like a line of white amongst the brown ridges and pulsating veins of his manhood.

Both trousers and shorts were now pulled down to his knees as he sat there on the edge of the bed, nervously waiting for her next course of action.

Gingerly, she took the cock in her hand and held it towards her waiting lips. Her tongue extended and made contact with the smooth, odorous surface of his glans.

The man shuddered.

Montana adjusted her kneeling position and allowed her tongue to slowly linger over the tip of the man's penis, licking it clean with lingering delicacy. With a finger pressed gently against one of the cock's blue veins she could feel the man's heartbeat as she manipulated his genitals. He sighed.

Outside the drawn curtains of the window she heard the roar of a jet either landing or taking off on the nearby runway. Her other hand moved down into his heat and cupped his heavy, hairy balls, feeling his dampness.

Her mouth descended on him and she took the cock deep into her, lowering her face so that she could devour it it all in one hungry gulp. Still, the man's cock refused to harden. She sucked, she licked, she nibbled, chewed on his most sensitive skin, but the thick penis remained soft. It was like eating gum. Gristly, malleable, unresponsive.

She moved her face away from his crotch.

"Don't you like me doing this to you?" she asked him.

"No, it's nice," he said. "I'm sorry I'm not getting it up. Maybe because this was all too sudden. I don't know why."

He genuinely looked sorry, embarrassed even.

"So, what do you want me to do?" she asked.

He straightened his posture, cock now dangling downwards between his naked thighs.

"Would you undress for me?"

"OK."

He slid himself back onto the bed, and positioned himself with his back against a raised cushion and the headboard.

Montana rose from her kneeling stance, wiped her lips dry and straightened out to her full height. When she stood like this, she appeared even taller than her officially registered 5' 9".

Distractedly fingering his soft cock, the man watched as she unbuttoned her top and let it drop from her shoulders. She hadn't been wearing a bra, he was pleased to confirm. Her breasts were small, but perfectly round, pink-tipped, a delicate pale shade of pink against the lunar whiteness of her skin. She took both breasts in her hands, caressed them, kneaded them, both firm promontories in the atoll of her torso.

"They never get very hard," she indicated. "Even when I'm at my most aroused," she added, pointing to her nipples.

"Ah," was all he could respond, entranced by the vision of

those small but perfectly shaped breasts as they stood out against the pallid landscape of her upper body. Her eyes moved downwards, where he was still moving a couple of fingers up and down his cock, to no immediate effect.

Her hands moved to the fastening at the back of her skirt and loosened the small metal catch. The short skirt fell silently to the ground as if in slow motion.

The man on the bed caught his breath. A shudder moved up and down his flaccid cock.

Her legs went on and on. Long.

Shapely.

But, also, she had not been wearing knickers.

Just a flimsy, lacy garter belt circling her waist, like a black crown above her hips, with thin snakes of material extending downwards to hold up her sheer stockings. Montana stepped out of the skirt now lying on the hotel room's beige shag pile.

The man's eyes were drawn to her pubic delta where a thin carpet of carefully trimmed darker blonde curls surrounded and guarded her intimacy. He squinted, in an attempt to distinguish the shape, the pattern of her gash behind the curls.

She was damn beautiful, he reflected.

"So?" she questioned him, standing just a yard away from him now, clad in just her stockings and garter belt, legs slightly apart.

The man couldn't find the right words to answer her properly. Sounds just died in his throat as he kept on watching her.

"Do you want to fuck me or not?" she asked, with a trace of irritation in her voice. She could feel a draught from under the room's front door circling her bare ass.

"I'd like to, I'd love to," he answered. "But I can't." He looked down at his inert genitals and attempted a smile. "My plumbing doesn't appear to be working right now."

"Is it me?" she asked.

"No. Not at all, you look wonderful. It's just that, sometimes, it happens. Or rather it doesn't happen. Age maybe? I don't know why. Absolutely nothing to do with you, I assure you."

"There are pills for that, these days," she pointed out.

"I know. But you have to take them an hour or two before, I'm told. Anyway, how could I predict I'd be meeting you? You really look stunning," he said. "You take my breath away. Although I'm not using that as an excuse for my lack of performance," he said.

"I'm as sorry as you are," Montana said. Then, as an afterthought, she asked: "Is there anything you'd like me to do?"

"Come to the bed. I'd like to touch you."

She took a step nearer.

"You can't kiss me," she said.

"On the lips, you mean?"

"Yes."

She sat next to him.

"Do you want me to take the stockings off?"

"No. You can keep them."

He brushed his fingers through her hair, then hesitantly moved them down towards her shoulders and, for the first time, made contact with her skin. Pale and soft. And strangely vibrant. A thin sheen of sweat had appeared on her forehead, he noticed as his hand travelled across the vast expanse of her upper body and finally ended in her pubic thatch. She was very dry, but did not object when he slipped a finger inside her to experience her heat.

His cock began to gain some girth as he did so.

"Good," she said.

He pushed deeper inside her, until his knuckle reached her thin, fleshy outer lips.

"Can I smell you?" he asked.

"Of course," Montana said.

He slowly pulled his finger out and brought it to his nose and inhaled the aroma of her that still lingered.

"Hmmm, nice."

"Do you want me to take you in my mouth again?" she suggested, eager to see his penis grow to full-length and operative hardness.

"Yes."

Montana leaned over, stretched out on the bed, kneeled and placed her head between the man's thighs and opened her mouth to receive him. She began to suck diligently, alternating circular movements of her tongue over his tip, ever so gentle small bites where his circumcision scar was, and hungry swallowing lips circled around his shaft.

The man's breathing became more halting, but the piece of sex meat inside her mouth was still too malleable, only half tumescent. With his fingers in her hair, he pushed down on her scalp, inviting her to take him even deeper. Had he been fully functional, Montana guessed, he would have almost reached the back of her throat. She slid a finger under his ball sack, reached the crease of his arse and pushed it inside him. He shuddered as her nail forced its way through the sphincter muscle and his balls contracted inside the crinkled, fleshy bag.

"Jeez . . ." he muttered.

Still sucking away, she pushed her finger even deeper into him, feeling the response in the shaft she was chewing on, a deep pulsating throb increasing in speed.

"Jeez, oh jeez . . ." the man shouted and spurted violently into her mouth as he suddenly came.

The speed of his orgasm had taken her by surprise. He was still far from hard. She didn't know men could come without being totally erect. The stuff dribbled out of his pee-hole and her tongue tried to avert the gelatinous emission. But his hand kept her head down. He tasted bitter. She had never liked to swallow and tried to redirect the come into the hollow of her cheek, away from her throat. The last, warm drops hiccuped out of his cock. Her mouth was full and Montana held her breath in an effort not to swallow the man's ejaculate. She pulled her finger out of his arsehole and he finally released the pressure against the top of her head.

She disengaged her mouth from his cock, moved off the bed and walked across to the bathroom where she quickly spat the stuff out and washed her mouth out with cold water.

She stood straight and saw her face in the mirror. The lipstick had disappeared from her lips and she looked tired, she felt. Small wrinkles were beginning to surface on the side of her eyes, no doubt from all those sleepless nights when Vanessa had been teething. She looked farther down at her naked body. But her breasts were still good, she reckoned. Unmarked, unstretched. She hadn't breast fed. The doctor had said her milk was too thin. Maybe that's what happened to women with cold hearts, she imagined.

She was just about to sit on the toilet when the man walked in. His trousers were now back on.

They exchanged silent looks.

Montana boldly ignored his stare and sat herself down on the wooden oval of the toilet. She opened her legs wide, stretching the lacy strands of the garter belt holding up her stockings.

"I need to pee," she said.

He hesitated for a brief moment.

"Can I watch?" he asked her somewhat sheepishly. "You did say anything? Earlier."

"Sure."

He kept on staring, eyes fixed on her cunt. She dipped her finger into the crease, slid it across the moist opening, ungluing the hairs loosely stuck together, and parted her vaginal lips.

The man was transfixed. Inside the trousers, she saw, he was now quite hard and big, his cock straining against the material.

Montana peed.

The release of the warm liquid which had been storing up inside her felt almost orgasmic. She closed her eyes, and listened to the stream splash against the porcelain bowl. It seemed to go on forever.

Finally, there was no more and Montana opened her eyes. The man in the suit was still standing motionless by the sink.

"You could lick me clean," she suggested.

He eagerly agreed to her demand.

He promptly got down on his knees on the tiled floor and

buried his head between her thighs, his sideburns scratching against the rougher surface of her stocking tops and offered her his tongue as she held herself wide open and he briefly peered deep inside her fierce pinkness before tasting her.

Later, both back in the bedroom, the man watched her dress and soon she was again fully clothed, not a sign on her face of what had occurred earlier, like two business people in their finery at the end of a delicate set of negotiations, stiff and formal.

She picked up her small handbag from the floor where she had earlier dropped it and he pulled a heavy wallet from the right inside pocket of his suit jacket.

"How much?" he asked her.

A faint look of surprise spread across her so far impassive features.

"Nothing," she said.

"But..."

"I don't do it for the money," Montana replied coldly.

"I just thought . . ." he mumbled. "A hotel bar and all that, and you being so laconic . . ."

"I don't do it for the money," Montana repeated.

And made her way towards the door.

In the long hotel corridor, the hidden ceiling speakers were playing an easy listening version of "No One Compares to U" by Mantovani and his million-and-thirty-seven strings.

Some hours later, she was luxuriating in the green warmth of her bathtub, her baby girl frolicking between her legs amongst the bubble-bath foam that littered the surface of the water. Vanessa chortled as she moved the elusive bubbles from one end of the bath to the other, smothering her mother's partly submerged breasts. Outside, day was turning swiftly to night but the house was a haven of comforting heat, punctuated by the merry sounds of her child.

Adrienne daydreamed.

Images flowed. Uninvited. Out of control.

The first time her husband, that kind man, had touched her: in a dance-hall corner in the university social club.

Vague memories of the boys who had come before but who hadn't been allowed to go that far, or touch her as intimately or as long as she let him that night.

All a blur of faces. And lips.

Their wedding day. The college chapel. Their parents both glowering at each other for reasons now long forgotten. The white, dowdy dress that had belonged to her grandmother and that still didn't seem to fit her, even after all the alterations her mother had made.

The feeling that a crucial choice had been made, but also her total indifference to the developing situation. As if she was only a spectator in these pompous proceedings.

How her husband's new wedding haircut had looked so undignified: short, unsuitable and badly coordinated with the new chain store–bought store three-piece dark brown suit he was wearing.

She remembered the flowers and their dull assortment of colours. The confetti. The hired cars. The small mole on the priest's cheek as he spoke to them of fidelity, eternity, and all that jazz.

Seemed like yesterday.

How did whole years go by so fast, she puzzled? Thousands of nights; hundreds of indifferent fucks and kisses after the initial heat had just somehow faded away; millions of words said as part of endless talks, conversations, arguments, dialogues and now, thinking back, she couldn't remember a single memorable word he had said to her or that she had said to him.

"Mummy, the water's getting cold. Can we leave?" Vanessa asked, shaking Adrienne from her torpor.

"Of course, darling," she answered, forcing herself to rise from the tepid waters. She stepped out of the bathtub and lifted the child over, wrapping her in a large towel.

And realized she hadn't even soaped herself throughout the bath, had just basked in it without actually washing.

The front door slammed.

"It's me," her husband called out.

"We're up here. In the bathroom," Adrienne shouted.

He walked upstairs.

"Ah, how lovely, my two darlings together, my two incomparable beauties!"

Vanessa giggled and ran over to embrace him.

"So, how was your salsa class?" he asked her later in the kitchen, as she sliced the vegetables for the evening meal.

"Fine, just fine. I'm really becoming an expert at it. One day, you should join me there. You'd find it fun."

"A bit difficult during the day," he said, pulling the tab from a beer can.

"I promise I'll keep an eye out for vacancies on the evening weekday schedule, if you're really interested," she suggested.

"Maybe," he muttered, sipping from the cold can.

Adrienne emptied the vegetables into the pan and asked:

"Are you planning on using the computer tonight?"

He had recently taken to using hers, as his had been crashing.

"No. Don't you remember? I'm meeting my brother for a drink?"

"Oh, yes. I do, now. Good, I should have prepared some new spreadsheets today, for the weekly new business meeting at the bank. Do you mind if I stay home and work on them?"

"Yeah, sure. Paulette isn't coming either, one of her night classes," he answered. "No problems. I won't be home too late. We're doing that presentation for that potential big new client from Chicoutimi in the morning, so I want to be in top form."

The vegetables in the pan began sizzling in the hot butter.

❐

Child sound asleep. The silence of night punctuated by the muted, distant laughter of neighbours watching sitcoms in nearby houses and the infrequent screech of brakes and tires on the highway.

Montana sat in the darkness of the upstairs study, her face bathed in the blue light of the computer screen.

Online. Not her usual hour. So many new, unfamiliar names. No one she knew. As if a new species of chat room addicts only came out at night, like vampires in a horror tale.

Time and time again, Montana scanned the ever-changing list as new handles appeared at the stroke of a distant keyboard, only to disappear an instant later to be replaced by still other new names. The rate of turnover was so rapid, and so many more people seemed only to be on at night. American time. Few Europeans in all likelihood, only insomniacs.

As she hesitated about taking the first step and calling up a total stranger, she received a "call."

She moved the mouse along the screen.

Christopher: Hi! Care to talk?

She began typing.

Montana: Hi. How are you?
Christopher: I'm fine. I've never been to Montana, but friends have told me the landscapes are wonderful.
Montana: So I'm told. It's just my name. I don't live there.
Christopher: OK. U m or f?
Montana: f
Christopher: Here for just chat, or fun or forlorn hopes of romance?
Montana: A combination of them all, I reckon.
Christopher: How old are you?

Montana: 32

Christopher: Married?

Montana: Yes.

Christopher: Alone right now?

Montana: Yes, we're in the process of separating.

Christopher: I'm sorry.

Montana: No need to be sorry for me. It's better that way.

Christopher: So where are you?

Montana: Here.

Christopher: (smile) I mean geographically?

Montana: Boston

Christopher: I'm in New York.

Montana: A flight away …

Christopher: (grin) indeed!

Montana: What do you do?

Christopher: I'm in sales. Equities and insurance. I travel quite a bit. You?

Montana: I don't travel at all (sigh).

Christopher: No, I meant what do you do? Housewife?

Montana: Real estate.

Christopher: That's interesting.

Montana: No, it isn't.

Christopher: OK, so it isn't. So, tell me what you're wearing?

Montana: A thin short-sleeved white T-shirt and jeans. No bra under, I'm small-breasted. Don't need one.

Christopher: I like small breasts. Underpants?

Montana: Black. Lacy. And also short white socks.

Christopher: Very nice. Tell me a bit what you look like?

Montana: I'm 5ft 4. Medium-length dark straight hair, brown eyes, small boobs (u know that already), long legs, thin, a curvy arse.

Christopher: Sounds very appetising. Are you feeling wet?

Montana: Not quite yet.

Christopher: I'm sitting here with my trousers loosened. I'm already quite hard. Do you want to cyber?

Montana: Sure.

Christopher: Good. Pull your T-shirt off.

Montana: OK, I've slipped it off.

Christopher: Touch your breasts. Twist your nipples between your fingers. Are they hard?

Montana: Yes, very.

Christopher: Wonderful. Now, Montana, stand up from your chair and undo your jeans and pull them down all the way to your ankles. Don't take them off completely, leave them bunched around your ankles.

Montana: Should I still keep my underpants on?

Christopher: I don't know. Do you want to take them off? Are you very wet? Can you see the wetness through the material.

Montana: Yes.

Christopher: I'm so hard for you already. Do you want to taste my fat cock?

Montana: Is it cut or uncut? How big?

Christopher: Uncut. 8 and a half inches. And right now straining at the leash. Big enough for you?

Montana: Sounds nice.

Christopher: Oh, yes, baby, really nice. Come, take it between your lips. Let me feel you swallow it.

Montana: OK, I have it in my mouth now. Gee, it is big, fills me completely, almost makes me choke.

Christopher: Suck on it, Montana.

Montana: I am.

Christopher: Do it faster, Montana baby. Faster, now. Oh, it feels so good.

Montana: I'm sucking faster. Hmmm, it tastes nice.

Christopher: While you're sucking me, baby, slip a couple of fingers into your slit and wank away. Tell me what it feels like.

Montana: But I still have my knickers on!

Christopher: Use your bloody imagination, girl. Hurry.

Montana: I'm sucking as hard as I can manage, catching my breath while I lick your balls …

Christopher: Yes. Yes. That's it. Do it. Quick, I'm going to come very soon, now. What about you? Are you dripping down there yet. Tell me what your fingers are doing … Tell me …

Montana: Listen, I've only a finite number of fingers. I still have to type all this shit, you know.

Christopher: Hell. Don't spoil it now, Montana. I'm just about to come. Tell me how you feel, PLEASE …

Montana: Can I just ask you one thing first?

Christopher: Yes, what? Hurry.

Montana: I was wondering if you are also married. Are you?

There was no immediate answer.

<Christopher has left the forum>

Montana smiled wryly and rose to fetch a bottle of mineral water from the fridge. She was wearing her tartan pyjamas and fluffy slippers. On the way back, she checked up on her daughter who was sleeping peacefully in the cot. An angel of innocence at rest. Vanessa was growing; soon, it would be time to treat her to her first proper bed. By the time she returned to the computer, there were two other calls beckoning her to the screen.

She pondered briefly which to accept.

Black stud: Hi there. Are you f?

m for f (fone sex): Interested?

Either would do.

Montana: F. All of me.

Black stud: All of you? Sure you're not a bloke? That's the sort of thing a bloke would say. Lotsa phonies here and I don't want to waste my time.

Montana: Genuinely f. You'll have to take that on trust, friend.

Black stud: Have a photo?

Montana: Have a lot of them, but no scanner. Anyway, would have to know you much better before I sent one, even if I could.

Black stud: So, want to talk then?

Montana: Sure. Why do you think I accepted your call? It wasn't the only offer, you know.

Black stud: Ever tasted black meat, cowgirl?

Montana: Don't think I have. So what makes it so different?

Black stud: Everything.

Montana: Everything? Tell me more, this gal's curious.

Black stud: Quality. Taste. Length. Staying power. Color. Size. You just haven't lived until you've tried black meat!

Montana: Quite a menu! So, where are you?

Black stud: Brixton, London.

Montana: Must be middle of the night there?

Black stud: Yeah. And you, you're a Yank, no?

Montana: Sort of. I'm American, but I live in Paris. Work here.

Black stud: Also sleepless, hey? Horny?

Montana: Rather.

Black stud: So, tell me, are you blonde, big tits, corn fed?

Montana: Blonde, yes. Quite voluptuous.

Black stud: How old?

Montana: 29. Another year and I'll be over the hill …

Black stud: So, do you like to fuck?

Montana: Sure. Divorced a year ago and moved to Paris. French guys are not all they're reputed to be. I sample one from time to time when hygiene calls!

Black stud: So, d'ya think you could take all of me?

Montana: I'd only know that if I tried, wouldn't I?

Black stud: There's a lot of me, girl.

Montana: Try me.

Black stud: Maybe I will at that, Montana. All holes. Stretch you a bit.

Montana: You'd be quite welcome.

Black stud: That's the spirit, girl … Tell you what, it's only a few hours to Paris. There's a Eurostar at seven or so in the morning. I could be fucking your white arse to kingdom come as early as eleven.

Montana: A fascinating thought …

Black stud: So?

Montana: So what?

Black stud: You sound like an adventurous lady; I have a good buddy, a pile driver of a cock. Ever thought of trying two guys?

Montana: Together?

Black stud: Yeah, just like in the porno movies. One in front, one in your rear.

Montana: What about my mouth, then? A bit of a waste leaving it unused (smile).

Black stud: Oh, don't you worry, you little slut, we'd manage to put those sweet lips of yours to very good use too! That's a promise.

Montana: Is that a dare?

Black stud: Say the word and I'm halfway to Paris, girl …

The downstairs door slammed. She hadn't heard her husband park his Volvo. Maybe the usual parking place outside their door had been taken. She quickly clicked her way out of the chat line and switched off the computer.

"Still up?"

"Yes, I was just about to go to bed."

"Managed to complete the spreadsheets?"

"Oh, those? Yes. No problem."

"Vanessa OK?"

"Yes, not a sound."

In the heart of the Montreal night, Montana tossed and turned repeatedly in their king-size bed. Sleep wouldn't come. Again. Like so many other nights. Thoughts cascading over each other with the dizzying speed of an acid trip (she had tried once, at university), unformed ideas, fuzzy images, and fragments of consciousness jostling desperately for her attention. Nothing appeared to make sense any longer inside her head.

Inside her body, on the other hand, confusion of another kind reigned.

She felt an immense heat within the emptiness, a flaming black hole which threatened to consume her whole, devouring her soul with avid relish, feasting greedily on her mixed-up emotions and feelings.

The body called.

The brain somehow reacted.

But they spoke a different language and no genuine connection was being established.

Or none that would make sense to her, at any rate.

Her earlier image, her reflection in the hotel mirror came back to her. Yes, she knew she was attractive. Men were seduced by her outward appearance. An illusion? Chemistry? Why did they fall in love with her so damn easily? It just wasn't fair. All her online lovers and their protestations of ardent desire, irredeemable lust and passionate longing, even those who didn't even know what she really looked like. It was a curse, she decided. Punishment for something bad, something wrong she must have done a while back. But she couldn't recall precisely what.

And here they all were, battering the ramparts of her mind as she reached out for the blessed relief of sleep. The one in New York who no longer called; the German guy in Berlin whose wife had died last year and promised to take her anywhere in the world if only she e-mailed him her photograph, and assured her he didn't even want sex, could live without it; the Israeli software expert who thought she lived in Seattle and begged her repeatedly for an address, a meeting whenever he was in town; the sundry Frenchmen; a lawyer; a businessman; a bi-sexual poet; all guaranteed bliss eternal at the drop of their trousers and a good meal. The girls, women out there who tried to draw her into lesbian encounters . . .

And Martin in London. The only one she had sent her photo to. The one taken on the beach, looking sleek and tall in the water off Palm Beach in her black one-piece swimming costume. Her hair tousled by the wind and her face partly obscured by her sunglasses. Martin, who had a sweet way with words and a penchant for melancholy as he alternated their dialogue with smooth seduction, welcome humor and sad moments of yearning.

She assured him of love but he insisted it wasn't enough.

Damn it—she pulled the covers up to her chin—why did men fall so easily in love with women who found it so difficult to love them back properly, like in books and the movies?

Montana momentarily faded into the blurry zone between sleep and reason, but an image of her childhood brought her back involuntarily to the room, the bed, the uncertainties.

She was six and the family had taken her to the mountains somewhere up north. She remembered the Japanese-like snowcapped tops littering the horizon as far as her small eyes could see. She was playing with her dolls in the backyard of the log cabin her parents had rented. Montana closed her eyes, blocked out the Montreal night, her gently snoring husband and the walls, the wooden house that surrounded her. First the smells of the forest drifted back, then the distinctive noises of birds and insects chirping away madly in full stereo all around her. She had a favorite doll, a raggedy one with orange hair, and would give her a different name every few days as she so easily got bored with each of them in succession. Names she would hear in stories read to her at school or in bed at night by her mother, names she would hear out of the corner of one ear from the television.

The doll was old. She had been taking it to bed for a couple of years as a comforter of sorts. There were a series of outfits for the battered toy, and her principle fun was to change the doll's clothes continuously, trying new combinations and variations in her attire. The doll's eyes were two shiny large, black buttons, sewn into a white circle and topped by a fringe of brown, woollen eyebrows.

One of the buttons had come loose. It happened often, and Montana's mother would always laugh when the child initially cried and quickly reassure her, while showing her how easy it was to sew the button, the doll's eye, back on.

"Brand new again," she would say and kiss Montana's forehead as she returned the salvaged doll to her.

As she pulled a piece of pink cotton that passed for a shirt over the doll's head, the loose button had snagged and the eye was once again torn from its fragile socket. These days, this no longer made Montana cry. She was a growing girl, as everyone in the family kept saying to her. Calmly, she picked the doll up and made for the cabin.

The radio was on in the kitchen and the little girl resolutely followed its sounds. Her mother must be cooking. Already the smell of food being prepared wafted up towards her nostrils, easily erasing the scent of the pine and invigorating fresh mountain air outside still lingering in her nose and lungs.

They hadn't heard her mocassin steps approach.

Her father must have returned through the back door. Montana hadn't seen him arrive. The car was parked a hundred yards below where the trail to the cabin began.

Her parents were kissing.

Montana held her breath and watched them for what seemed like ages. They were standing by the cooker, her father's hands roaming across her mother's back, mouth against mouth, body tightly against body, silent. Were it not for the movement of his hands, they could have been statues.

Both had their eyes closed.

The kiss went on for ever.

Finally, Montana must have moved or coughed, they opened their eyes and realised the child was there. They smiled and acknowledged her.

"Hello, sweetie pie," she thought she remembered one of them saying.

And, noticing her quizzical look, the other said: "Don't worry. We're in love, that's all."

And they both laughed.

Montana silently proffered her injured doll.

Her memory drifted back from childhood to confusion. Images danced around. Thoughts took a roller-coaster ride through illogical maps of unreality and the topography of dreams took over.

She closed her eyes and found sleep.

Lunch hour. The next day.

"I'm staying in," she said to Deborah. "I've brought sandwiches. I'll see you later."

Her colleague walked towards the elevator and Montana closed the door to her office. The next meeting was not until three that afternoon.

She entered her password into the desktop computer and soon clicked her way through to the Intimate Chat Forum.

mk: welcome.

Montana: Hi and how are you today?

mk: Much the same as usual. And you, do anything interesting on your day off?

Montana: Just my salsa class.

mk: How I'd love to be able to see you dance.

Montana: You should learn to. Find a club or somewhere, and watch all the pretty women as they move around so gracefully and just imagine that the prettiest of them all is me!

mk: I've been thinking of you a lot.

Montana: Have you? You surprise me (smile).

mk: Too much.

Montana: Why too much, there's never too much?

mk: There is.

Montana: What do you mean?

mk: I don't know if I should tell you. Maybe you'll think badly of me, Montana.

Montana: ?

mk: Well, you know I changed my handle the other month?

Montana: Yes, instead of Marty you now use your initials ...

mk: I was getting too many calls from guys who thought I was f. They were all thinking of Martina, I suppose, rather than Martin.

Montana: Yes, I remember. Have the initials helped?

mk: A little.

Montana: So?

mk: It's stupid. All this Internet chat, these false hopes of meeting someone, looking for sex and all that, it's crazy. Puts ideas into your head.

Montana: What sort of ideas?

mk: Makes you think. Wonder. You know me, I'm curious about the way other people live, I try to understand what makes them tick. Especially you.

Montana: (smile)

mk: There are all these handles about, bi people seeking this or that ...

Montana: I see them, too. It's strange how many people here seem to be bisexual by nature. I wonder if they're all telling the truth. You know there are so many who pretend to be what they're not.

mk: Yes. Anyway, it set me thinking. I was just curious, you see. On occasions, I must confess I called up some bi women, but none of them seemed to be interested in talking. Only keen on their own kind, I suppose. I just wanted to talk. Then yesterday, oh Montana, forgive me, my curiosity got the better of me.

Montana: And?

mk: I called up a bi m.

Montana: !

mk: We talked a bit. Maybe I played along with him a bit. OK, so

I pretended I was also bisexual ... he happened to be local and, it's mad, I agreed to meet him ...

Montana: You had sex with him???

mk: Yes, well no. Not completely. He sucked me and I also sucked him. Well, I've been sucked by women and I thought it was only fair to find out what doing it to a man would feel like. That's all. We didn't have proper sex. We didn't even exchange names.

Montana: I'm fascinated, Martin. Shocked but fascinated. So what did it feel like taking another man's penis in to your mouth?

mk: Difficult to explain really. Somewhat different to what I expected. Not so firm. Even a bit rubbery. Can't say I liked it, but neither did I dislike it. That surprised me.

Montana: Did you swallow?

mk: No. We'd agreed beforehand and he came outside my mouth. Me too. I'd warned him I was quite new to this and not quite ready for it. He didn't seem to mind. It was just curiosity, I assure you, Montana. Now that I know, it'll probably never happen again.

Montana: Probably?

mk: Never. Can I ask you a question?

Montana: Go ahead.

mk: Does your husband often ask you to suck him off? Do you enjoy it?

Montana: You're breaking the rules, Martin. You know that talk of my family is strictly out of bounds.

mk: Yes. I'm sorry.

Montana: I have a question for you, though. My turn to be curious.

mk: Yes?

Montana: Where did it happen? Did you both undress for it?

mk: We went to his flat. A bit of a depressing place. A bed-sit. Yes, we both undressed completely. It was my idea. The thought of just pulling our cocks out and remaining dressed for the proceedings was just too sordid to contemplate.

Montana: OK.

mk: Do you think any the worse of me, Montana?

Montana: Not at all. I understand you. With all the time we both waste online, it just puts ideas into your head. God, I do understand you.

mk: What are we searching for here, hey?

Montana: You tell me.

mk: But the experience also reminded me of how much I miss you. I want you so badly, Montana.

Montana: I know, Martin. But we can't do anything about it.

mk: Why?

Montana: Because if we allowed it to happen, it would spoil everything.

mk: Again I ask you: why?

Montana: It just would.

mk: We're going round in circles, again.

Montana: It seems like it.

mk: I have a visitor here in a few minutes, I'll have to go. Tomorrow? Same time, same place?

Montana: Tomorrow.

Another dimly lit narrow hotel corridor festooned with doors like pictures in an exhibition. Blue Monday. The airport Hyatt Regency.

"So your name is O and you'll fuck for free? Is it O for Ophelia?"

"I said I'd fuck you for free," Montana answered as he slotted the electronic card into the door's shiny metal jaw. "And by the way, it's just O for O . . ."

"I've got cash, you know, a lot, not just credit cards. Real money. US dollars, French Francs, Sterling, Bahts, Italian Lira. I go all over the place. You sure there's nothing some extra money can buy, maybe?"

"No," Montana replied. "I told you earlier at the bar that I will be all yours for an hour. But I won't kiss. That's the only proviso, the only cost to you."

They entered the hotel room.

The customary landscape of tidy, predictable anonymity.

He moved the laminated "Do Not Disturb" sign onto the outside handle and carefully locked the door behind him.

Montana dropped her handbag to the floor.

"What do you keep in there, O?" the man asked.

"My car keys, lipstick, a bit of a cash. Nothing much," she said.

"No mace spray, condoms?"

"No."

"Isn't that a bit imprudent?" he queried.

"Why should it be?"

"I could be anybody."

"I chose you, I go by gut instinct. At worse you'd only rape me. But then why did I come to this room with you for?" she smiled.

"I suppose so," he said. "But I haven't condoms either. Don't travel prepared for this sort of encounter, you know."

"I'm on the pill," she answered.

"What about diseases?"

"I'll trust you if you trust me. Anyway, don't we both look just the epitome of middle-class professionals?"

"I still don't understand why you won't take cash," the man said, slipping his sports jacket off and loosening his tie.

"I don't need it," Montana said.

"Maybe the incentive of money could inspire you to something special?" he insisted.

"I said anything," she reminded him again.

He shrugged and moved closer to her. A mile away a jumbo landed noisily on a snow-surrounded runway. He touched her cheek with a lone finger, cupped her chin with the hollow of his hand and, applying gentle pressure, forced her to raise her head and look him in the eyes.

Atoll green into dark brown.

"I don't understand you," he said, fixing her.

She held his gaze.

"I don't understand myself sometimes," she replied.

She could hear the sound of his breath and feel his body heat. He lowered his hand and unbuttoned her white silk shirt. He moved to her breasts and deftly lifted both out of the black bra. Her nipples hardened as he touched them, fingertips lingering on their puckered peaks.

"Aren't Wonderbras flattering?" she whispered ironically as the modest size of her liberated breasts was revealed.

The man didn't reply but smiled quietly.

He suddenly brought his lips towards her face, but she quickly turned her cheek to avoid the contact he sought.

"No."

"Bitch."

"I said anything but that," she confirmed as the man breathed hard against her face, his peppermint smell running across her cheeks. "Why do men always want what they can't have?"

He buried his tongue into her right ear, licking, exploring, delicately chewing on her lobes. The tingle inside Montana rose violently as he did so, unknowingly activating one of her most erogenous zones which even her husband had always somehow avoided.

The man felt her response and, cruelly, withdrew; he stepped back a few feet, a look of anger, or was it frustration painted across his ruggedly irregular features. Aquiline nose. High forehead. Short light brown hair.

"Undress," he ordered her.

His voice had sharpened.

Montana stripped, peeling off the trouser-suit jacket, completed unbuttoning the white silk blouse and unzipped the trousers, which fell to the floor. She looked at the man now watching her. His look was impassive but impatient.

"The rest," he commanded her.

She pulled the bra round from which her breasts were

already pouring and undid its clasp. The thin garment floated to the carpet. She bent over and slipped the white bikini panties down and straightened out, now fully naked for the man's delectation. He neither commented on her appearance nor reacted.

"Do you . . . ?" she began saying.

"Shut up," he shouted at her. "I don't want to hear a further word out of you unless I ask you something. Understood?"

"But . . ."

He glowered.

"No buts or ifs, just keep your mouth shut. OK?"

She meekly nodded, all of a sudden feeling particularly vulnerable to his undeserved wrath.

As she stood there, her body heat decreased and she began feeling the cold from outside seep into the hermetically sealed hotel room. She waited for what would inevitably come next.

Finally, following a few minutes of pensive hesitation, the man began undressing, hurriedly, untidily scattering his clothes where they fell. His lean body emerged, flat stomach, utterly hairless chest as if he depilated himself, strong thighs, an athlete's calves, long thin erect cock already poised at an angle of attack over a heavy ball sack, a caramel brown tan emphasised by the white band across his waist and genitals.

Montana couldn't help herself and remarked:

"You've recently been somewhere warm and exotic, I see. Vacation?"

"Yes, an island," he replied. Then, remembering his previous orders, "And not another bloody word from you or else. Understood?"

Why did her words, an attempt at polite interface for what was after all a sad, sordid episode, annoy him so much, Montana wondered?

He threw his socks across the room and walked over to face Montana. His hands quickly roamed all over her, testing the tautness of her stomach, the firm curves of her arse, exploring the warmth of her slit. As he pressed against her, his unfurled cock flattened itself against her stomach, nesting, probing. He spun her round, seemingly examining every revealed square inch of her, like a doctor, noting every little blemish on her skin, small birth marks, a few darker moles, the angle of her softness, the visible reef of her vertebrae across the flat landscape of her back. His fingers barely skimmed the surface of her skin as they continued to explore her in full detail, inspecting his merchandise; and the playful come and go of his touch began to arouse her senses. She felt like begging him to stay in one spot a bit longer, more here, even more there so that she might feel the tide rise out of control within and the waves of pleasure increase their languorous ebb and flow deep inside her. But somehow, the man sensed this and continued his halting journey across her.

Finally, he took a few steps back and stood there frowning.

Montana interpreted this as encouragement, an indication that she could now begin the private dance that led to sex. She moved up to him and took a hold of his long, thin penis and made to kneel, licking her lips as she did so in anticipation of his offering.

But the man reacted suddenly to this, and slapped her on the cheek with the back of his hand. Montana gasped in surprise, the cock slithered out of her hands and she stumbled back against the edge of the bed. It stung. Before she could open her mouth and protest , the man screamed angrily at her:

"Oh no, you don't, you bitch. Don't touch me there! I just want to fuck you, that's all! I know your kind, you think a quick blow-job would do it quicker, see me spend myself before I can do it to you. No way."

Montana knew there was no point replying. She massaged her cheek where he had struck her. The imprint of his knuckles was still warm.

"Now!" he ordered loudly.

Montana got back on her feet and, somewhat scared by the

developing situation, retreated onto the bed. If this was what the man wanted, they might as well get it over with.

"No," she heard him roar again.

She questioned him silently, her green eyes all watery by now.

"Not on the bed."

The anger in him appeared to have made its way down to his cock, its head now engorged with dark red rage, surging away from his body like an independent appendage altogether.

Perched on the end of the bed, legs akimbo, open wide in a most obscene way, Montana indicated her puzzlement.

He moved to her, seized her by the arm, gripped her with cruel force and pulled her away from the bed. She stumbled.

"On the floor!" he ordered. "NOW! And on your knees . . ."

She positioned herself as he wanted her, rump high, the apex of her thighs at its most extreme, revealing every dark inch of her intimacy, feeling now more vulnerable than ever as he positioned himself behind her and, without a word of warning, brutally entered her in one movement, burying himself deeply inside her while his free hand savagely pulled her arse cheeks apart until the pull on the skin hurt her badly.

Now inside her, stretching her as she had seldom been manipulated before due to the degrading position he had forced her in, the man began his in and out thrusts. In, he buried himself in her warm depths to the very hilt, balls slapping against the pallor of her raised arse; out, he reversed back, pulling her insides with him due to the lack of lubrication, until only his cockhead remained submerged in her.

Then in again and out again. And again.

He pumped along for an eternity, like clockwork and with a strength quite totally devoid of the slightest delicacy.

It wasn't sex, it was a battle.

For him Montana was no longer a woman, she was flesh, she was meat, there to be used. As he savagely moved inside her and repeatedly pulled at her arse cheeks until she knew the crease would be red for days, she tried to control her tears, and mentally began counting the cadence of his steady assault.

"Say something, bitch. Moan, cry, something," he said, as he worked on her.

But Montana refused. This was one pleasure she would not provide him with.

He realised this, and as suddenly as he had thrust himself into her, he pulled out altogether, sucking the air out of her vagina as he did and slapped her rump repeatedly in an attempt to evince a reaction from her.

Montana bit her tongue.

"No reaction, hey?" he said. "Maybe if I fucked you in the arse, I'd hear you squeal at last, would I?"

As he said this, he positioned his cock at the opening of her anus and, with all his pelvic strength, pushed. However thin he was, the barely wet cock foundered against the outer ring of her hitherto unpracticed sphincter muscles. But where he had struck, she could already feel a deep bruise and the concentric whirlpool of pain extending throughout her body.

"Bitch!"

He tried again.

Failed.

"Cunt!"

At his next attempt, some pre cum oozed out of his cock and he slid against her and flopped against her arse. Again, in anger, he smacked her repeatedly. She could only imagine how red her backside must now be.

"Shit!"

Montana clenched her teeth, tightened all her rear muscles to resist what she knew would be his final attempt to breach her. It was now a question of pride that he would not fuck her there. No way. Enough was enough.

He positioned himself at her opening and pressed once more as hard as he could, but the cock could find no hold in the puckered crater of her anus to get a grip on and buttress its entry. The friction became too much, and as the man gulped, he came. His come burst out and splattered across her back and scarlet cheeks.

The man moaned and writhed, leaning over her, dripping.

Montana, still undignified and open on all fours, finally summoned the will to talk again:

"Is that what you wanted?" she asked him.

"You fucking bitch! You bloody whore!" the man muttered under his breath, his cock now drooping pathetically, spent, out of action. He rose to his feet, straightened up and now towered over Montana's prone body.

For a brief moment, she feared he might exact revenge for his maddening frustration by pissing on her. Nothing would have surprised her now. From him. From men.

But the stranger she had picked up in the hotel bar did surprise her after all.

He walked away from her. She changed her position so that she was now squatting on the carpet, almost provoking him by displaying the split, gaping lips of her cunt, as she felt sensation returning to her wrists and knees. The man picked up Montana's clothes and, with rage, curled them all up in a bundle, bent over to retrieve her handbag, opened it and stuffed the crumpled items partly into the bag.

"Out!" he ordered her. "Out now . . ."

Montana acquiesced.

"If that's the way you want it. OK. I'll just have to clean myself up in the bathroom first."

She rose from the floor, but before she had caught her balance, the angry man had moved across to her, thrown the handbag and its dangling clothes against her and gripping her arms pushed her towards the door. As he unlocked the hotel room door, Montana attempted a backward movement, but the door opened and with all his strength the man pushed her out into the corridor. She tried to halt her expulsion by moving her leg against the door but he gave her a savage kick and she was obliged to retreat.

In the narrow corridor, Montana stumbled, naked, his come still pearling down her back. There was, fortunately, no witness to her distress. She hurriedly slipped her clothes on and took the elevator straight to the basement car park.

Not her best day, she wryly reflected.

"Where did you get that bruise on your thigh?" her husband asked that evening as they prepared for bed.

"Caught it against the edge of my desk at the office last week. You know how clumsy I am."

"Strange. I don't recall noticing it over the weekend."

"Not so strange, darling. You seldom look at me when I'm naked these days, do you? Anyway, I bruise so easily."

Miles and Miles

Often at night as spring approached and the snows melted at last, Montana would dream awake of the lives she had never had. Or would never have. Strange how sometimes the slightest thing would evoke images, thoughts, ideas unbidden: a new word Vanessa would use, learned at nursery school, the glimpse of a couple walking hand in hand in the avenue below her corner office window, the innocuous shrug of someone's shoulder during a planning or forecast meeting, the twist and turn of a melody on the scratchy speakers of her salsa class, the lengthening silence between Martin's messages when they spoke online (less frequently now, as he was often away on business somewhere in the wide world), the incongruous demands of her more explicit Internet interlocutors, or a reflection of her own face in the morning mirror. Another day, another Canadian dollar, life flowing calmly onwards like a river, floating, no longer in control of the steering wheel.

These were the bittersweet days when Montana asked herself all those questions that had no answers. Puzzled about the line she had read somewhere that queried whether life was all there was to living.

She knew she wanted more, and her vain efforts to change the course of events seemed just another foolhardy assault on windmills.

Maybe, she reflected—mentally switching off from the Citicorp May investment spreadsheets scattered across her desk—she was just too greedy. There, that was an easy answer. Be content with the small victories of life, Adrienne, and you will be happier, girl. But Montana could not accept this as an answer.

Time flows slowly, time flows quickly. Another day, another gentle marital fuck, another cuddle with a sweet child issued from her very flesh, more meals and conversations about the weather. Another day and another ration of emptiness. Jesus, her uncle the lawyer had even convinced her husband and herself to draw up wills, increase their respective contributions to their pension plans, simplify their mortgage options even though it still had nearly twenty years to go. It all felt like a trap. She wanted to scream that she was still young, or at least, still felt young. Was there a difference between being and feeling?

She no longer even looked forward to Monday. Salsa day. Hotel day. Montana comes alive day. Even madness can become a routine.

"You look a bit sad, these days," her husband had remarked one Sunday night. "Anything I should know. Problems at the bank?"

"No," Montana replied. "Just a bit tired. Don't you worry, I'll get over it."

"Good," he replied. "It's just that we haven't been talking much recently."

"Haven't we?"

"Well, not really."

She knew it already. A couple of weekends before she had actually counted how many words had passed between them on a Sunday spent together. Barely three hundred. According to an article she had read in a women's magazine, the average dialogue between husband and wife should reach at least fifteen words per intervention, so this was low indeed. She had mentioned it to Stephanie, who had conducted a similar experiment with her Telecom engineer husband of eight years and her friend had given up counting by midday, past a thousand words or so. And they didn't even get on too well, especially since he'd found out about her regular Friday after-work drink with a guy from her office who had wanted them to both run off to Tahiti together.

"I was thinking . . ." Pierre said hesitantly.

"Yes?"

"Vanessa is so lovely, such a great child. Maybe we should have another? Would you like that?"

"Maybe," Montana had replied, quite unprepared for this novel subject. "Let's talk about it again in a few weeks."

Montana gave up her salsa class and tried other dances and other schools.

It sometimes meant different clothes and much of the pleasure involved the shopping, the trying on of gaudy new garments in exiguous shop cabins, the initial sensation of new material against skin, the movement a roll of her hip or shoulders would impress on the garment as it grew familiar with the round planes of her body in motion.

Her tango partner was a thin man in his mid-fifties who always wore black from head to toes: shoes, socks, trousers, shirt, even tie. His name was Raoul and she sensed something foreign about him, in his fluent steps, a kind of animal grace.

Sipping a drink of cold water halfway through one session, she had asked him once: "Raoul, tell me a bit about your life. I'd like to know. Really."

"We're here to dance, Montana. That's all," he answered. "What you truly wish to know is about the women in my past life, isn't it?"

She lowered her eyes and nodded affirmatively, blushing slightly. A hole in one!

"That's private. Very private. My stories only belong to me. And to them."

She wanted to understand the life of others.

Faced by the repeated lack of response, Montana danced.

Lost herself in it.

She moved across the wooden dance floors like a mermaid across the ocean, rocks scattered amongst choppy seas and reefs. She glided. She swam. Like a boat. Like a woman.

Her body adhered to the varying rhythms of the music, swaying with the melody, fighting the beat, always halfway between grace and disequilibrium as she fought the spell of gravity in her attempt to marry the sound of the dance with sensual precision.

She danced.

With or without partners.

Most often, she was the youngest woman in her classes, a beacon of agility and fire amongst the pensioners and idle who were only here to kill time or recall memories of their youth. When Montana danced, there was never enough time. It was there to be seized before it disappeared, faded inexorably into the fold of a dance tune never to be recaptured.

Her instructors complimented her on her energy and strength, but urged more technical control, less abandon. But as soon as one step was mastered, she would hurriedly move on to another. Because she knew all too well that even in the heart of each dance, as she stepped, swirled, sidestepped, melted into the music, her body was never really in unison with her movements. It was a few degrees off, beating at the walls of a parallel universe, the one she was maybe attempting to reach through the sweat and pain and whose existence she was beginning to doubt. Following each Monday dance class, she would invariably orbit towards the airport hotels, sometimes without even showering. The men did not mind, it wasn't the acrid smell of her dance floor perspiration, it was her body, her apertures they sought. Some were even turned on in a major way by the strong, uncommon animal fragrance.

So they fucked her regardless.

She gave the gift of her body to strangers, until their faces and bulging cocks all blurred in her mind and she accepted them inside her with indifference, her mind on standby, a spectator at her defilement. And soon, even the airport encounters became predictable. Boring. Men of so little imagination. Two or three positions at most in their limited erotic vocabulary.

A paso doble class completed. She drove to the French side of town and its most shady streets, infested with sex shops and porno movie houses. One or two of her female office friends actually whispered that they had brothels around there. She dreamt of them often and what happened inside those dark walls. Only healthy curiosity, she would tell herself when she awoke in the throes of a particularly obscene dream.

A peep show in the unmentionable *quartier*. The fat manager escorted her to a back room. The disagreeable smell of chemical disinfectant hovered over the whole premises. Canned music filtered like a drowning man's final bubbles of consciousness through speakers scattered in all corners of the seedy establishment. "Big Spender," "Satisfaction," "Michelle."

"I can dance," Montana told him.

"Can you, then?"

"Most Latin American dances in fact."

"Well, lady, that's not in much demand here."

"I understand."

"As long as you can move your bod a bit, that's all the punters want, really."

"I can."

"There's a rota. You have to spend half an hour at a time in the booth, and that includes private sessions . . ."

"Meaning?"

"Meaning one to one in a cabin with the client who requests you. What you do there for your tips is up to you."

"I see."

"A minimum of six shifts a day. More is up to you. If you're good, you move to evenings, it's busier. more generous tips. But you start on mornings or lunch, they all do, even the lookers. Have to pay your dues."

"I can only do Mondays," she pointed out.

"Piss poor day, Monday. You're not going to earn much just working then."

"It's all I'm willing to do," she pointed out.

"Fine," the fat man sighed. "So, let's see you . . ."

Montana hesitated, then understood what he was requesting.

"I want to see your body, girl," he confirmed. "Don't fret, I've seen enough skin in my time in this business. I won't touch you."

She had barely enough space to wriggle out of her clothes, pinned as she was between his desk and the back wall. He cleared an ashtray and a pile of old racing newspapers off his desk when he saw her looking for a space to put her clothes down on.

She straightened, arms akimbo, facing the manager of the peep show joint.

"You haven't got much up top, have you?" he stated.

"No," she agreed. "But they're firm . . ."

"Nice legs," he said. "Turn round a bit." She did, now facing the pocked wallpaper.

"Nice ass, a bit square. You're very pale, you know. Ever thought of using a tanning lamp?"

"No, I haven't."

"Some more color might suit you. You're too milky, porcelain-doll like. Tall doll, though," he sniggered. "You can turn round again."

He could feel his gaze lingering on her cunt as he kept on examining her in silence.

"So, can I work here?" she asked him. "I know what it entails and I'm quite ready for it, you know."

"Hands through the opening, touching you up for a few extra bucks, everywhere, fingers up you, and all that?" he questioned her. "And more. This is no fancy strip joint," he added. "It's a meat rack. Pure and simple. You have to understand that, Montana. No pretence. Skin for cash, that's what it's all about."

He saw her blanch. But she nodded in response nonetheless.

"I think I understand," he finally said. "You're in it for the kicks, aren't you lady? It's not the money you're after, just the thrill?"

Montana said nothing, beginning to shiver as the inhospitality of this fetid back room enveloped her.

"No, not really," he finally said following a further minute's silence. "I don't think it would work. You're too . . . normal. Girls here are not from your walk of life. I don't think you'd blend in well. Not our type. Sorry. Better get dressed again."

Driving home, dusk falling quickly across the industrial landscape of suburban Montreal, Montana breathed a profound sigh of relief. Maybe it was for the best, after all. But deep inside her she also knew that had the manager given her the nod, she would have been in that booth the following Monday, rouged to the hilt, fixed smile in place, her wares on display for the disembodied eyes on the other side of the flimsy peep show partition.

That evening, when her husband made gentle sexual advances in bed, she pretended her period was starting.

Weekday lunch break. Transfer to applications. Strangled buzz on the dedicated modem line. Password. Intimate chat line. Click on "Who's here".

Martin was here. All last week, she had noted the presence of his name on the list, but he had never called her. Too busy speaking to other women? Angry at her? Disappointed? Montana felt a twinge of remorse. He was the only one here who was not just an anonymous, ghostly voice on her computer screen.

But her pride prevented her from calling him, drawing attention to herself. Fear that he might not respond, thus signifying silently the end of their halting relationship.

The screen pinged.

Fesdu: Hi Montana!

She was about to acknowledge this new name when the screen came to life again and another rectangular field appeared, obliterating its predecessor.

mk: Hi. How are you today?

Montana: I'm fine. You? It's been some time, hasn't it?

mk: I've been busy. Business travel and all that.

Montana: And new friends?

mk: Yes, that, too. I'm sorry I didn't call you, but I just feared our dialogue would just go round in circles again and again and I was tired. Melancholy.

Montana: Did you miss me when you travelled?

mk: Yes. A lot.

Montana: How much, my sunshine?

mk: Enough to think of you and masturbate myself to sleep in those lonely hotel rooms.

Montana: I'm flattered. Do you imagine much of my body, do you?

mk: Too much, I dream forbidden dreams where I am the gust of air that passes silently between the bed sheets and your sleeping body. I glide through the valley between your breasts, the color of your eyes, the ravine of your navel just an indentation in your map before your stomach dips towards the flower of your cunt …

Montana: Hmmmm … How I like it when you say these things, my love. I do love you so much.

mk: Do you really? It's a very distant and detached sort of love.

Montana: But love nonetheless.

mk: Montana, I'm no longer even sure if you know what love really is.

Montana: Don't be cruel again, my Martin. I've told you enough times that you are inside my heart and always will be. Whatever happens.

mk: Quite right, nothing happens.

Montana: If you're going to be nasty to me again, I'll just log off, I warn you. I don't like it when you go all sarcastic.

mk: Irony, not sarcasm. Not the same thing, Montana.

Montana: Stop being so pedantic …

mk: Well, you know me, I'm just a poor man of words.

Montana: So, use those words, be a poet again. For me, Martin.

mk: Where was I, then? Yes, I had reached that holy of holy, your sweet cunt, your gash, your slit, just waiting there for my fingers to unfurl its darker lips and invade your inner pinkness and moisture ...

Montana: mmmmmmmm ...

mk: But I know I'm not allowed to linger, this is territory that belongs to another, your damn husband ... So my imagination continues its journey, on and on, intrepid explorer of your body. Your pale, quivering thighs and ...

Montana: You should see my thighs right now! I have so many bruises there, I'm spotted black, blue, and yellow!

mk: How come?

Montana: I'm too clumsy. Always catching the corner of my desk at work. It's only painful for a short while, but the bruises stay there for weeks.

mk: I see.

Montana: So, you never did send me that e-mail you'd promised telling me all about the two of us on a tropical beach, did you?

mk: My mind's not in the right frame of mood. I will, one day. I'd rather take you to a beach, an island, anywhere than imagine it, you know.

Montana: Your e-mails give me so much pleasure. I treasure them.

mk: Do you? Nice to know I've become a jerk-off aid when your husband can't perform satisfactorily.

Montana: Oh, that's so nasty, Martin! How could you say things like that?

mk: Sometimes, I can. Listen, can you hold on a minute? My phone is ringing. Won't be long.

Montana: OK.

As she waited, she began sorting out the mess of files piled up on the corner of her desk. Too many obsolete printouts and minutes of meetings she would never need to refer to any longer. A full ten minutes went by, occasionally interrupted by the ping of others seeking her conversation.

Montana: Are you still there?

Another five minutes. She was about to chase him again, when the line flashed across the screen.

<mk has left the forum>

"Damn and damn again," she muttered. But such were the ways of Netsex; you never knew whether something you had said had either shocked or disappointed your interlocutor, or if the communication breakdown was genuine or electronic, better prospects on another line or frozen screen, spouse or child walking in; or maybe even suicidal despair.

The clouds outside the bank window trooped across the sky in the shape of exotic ziggurats, layer upon layer embedded within each other, like a monstrous puzzle waiting to be solved by a perspicacious eye.

Montana stayed on for another twenty minutes of desultory fishing, both prey and bait, but nothing could hold her attention today.

"Are you bi? we are seeking bi f for a threesome," "How old are you, I'm into women over forty", "Are you undressed?", "Are you wet?", "How did you lose your cherry?", "Are you horny already?", "What is your favorite position?", "Ever watched two guys sucking each other off and then wanted to join in?", "Can I phone you?", "How big are your nipples?", "Would you touch yourself?", "Do you think you could take all of me?", "Are you pierced?", "How loud are you when you come?", "Guess where my tattoo is?", "Do you swallow?"

Questions, questions. The new rhetoric of sex. Not that much more different than the old, just via a different medium.

❐

Easter time. Chocolate eggs. Vanessa's noisy birthday party.
The Barbie doll and fancy wardrobe she had coveted bringing
out a beautiful gleam in her childish eyes. Family visits. A minor
crisis in the Investment department which had her working
several Mondays in a row, monitoring the market and the Far
Eastern turmoil. The Dow Jones zigzagged, the Nikkei plum-
meted before partly recovering, the FT ambled on like a steady
stream traversed by hiccups.

May. First flowers of spring blooming in the front garden.

Car serviced last week, engine purring like a contented cat as
she approached the spaghetti intersection of the regional highways which acted as a preface for the airport and its myriad
satellites.

Sheraton today. Montana wore her shocking red bolero top,
a short skirt, and sandals. The bar glittered with polished
chrome and her reflection bounced from glass tabletop to
mirrored ceiling and walls and back again. Not a place to get
drunk in—you wouldn't see double—more likely a whole
hockey team of alcoholic illusions in this shining hall of mirrors.

Half an hour went by without a likely target for her lust. A
German airline pilot had earlier given her a quizzical look. She
had held his gaze, but he had then ignored her and moved on to
his flight.

She was about to give up, when she heard a rustle of movement behind her.

"You're Montana, aren't you?"

He was an older man, late-fifties or early-sixties she guessed.
Meticulously dressed, hair white all over, poised, the cut of his
suit evoking Italian or French designer craft.

"Yes," she answered. This was the first time she had seen this
man. How could he know her pseudonym? But she did prefer
older men, she knew. More elegance, more experience, more
kinks.

"Montana, who haunts the airport bars and offers her body
for free," the older man smiled at her.

"Indeed," she answered, having decided to brazen this out as laconically as she could manage.

"I had heard about you, and was hoping we would meet."

"My fame is spreading, is it?" she said. "Maybe I should adopt another name . . ."

"But you do, don't you, and I'm sure Montana herself is just another mask, isn't it?"

"A girl needs some element of privacy."

"Don't worry, young woman, I have no desire to discover your real name. It's not important."

He sat down in the upholstered armchair next to her.

"You are indeed very pretty," he said. "I have not been lied to."

"I come recommended by an earlier customer, do I?" she asked him.

"By several."

She wondered briefly what it would feel like to be fucked by this man. He would be rough, he would be hard, she guessed, but attentive, sensual.

"Do you have a room here?" she queried.

"No."

"I won't go anywhere else," she quickly said. "Away from here, I'm another person. But if you get yourself a room, I will come with you."

"That's not what I desire. As much as the prospect of making love to you holds much allure."

"What do you want with me, then?"

"More."

A mad thought crossed her mind briefly.

"You're not with the police, are you? What I do is not illegal, I never take money . . ."

"And neither am I with hotel security, although if I were you I would be wary of them. You haven't gone unnoticed," he interrupted her.

Montana took a sip from her sunrise cocktail and composed herself.

"I'm listening."

"I come with a proposal I think might interest you."

"A proposal?"

"I think I know why you pick up men in places like this, Montana. You are seeking something, but it's too intangible and you don't even know if it even exists. I think I can help. You're married, aren't you?"

"Yes."

"Find a pretext and free yourself for one whole week."

"That's not easy."

"I'm sure you can find a way."

"Maybe." She had accumulated quite a lot of overtime. The bank would no doubt prefer extra vacation days to be taken in lieu rather than pay her.

"If it's sex and new sensations and answers to all those questions your mind and body are constantly bombarding you with, we can help, Montana."

"We?"

He ignored her.

"All we ask is one week of your life and your total trust. You will come to no harm and derive much pleasure from the experience, I think. Just one week. Is that a lot to ask?"

"I suppose not."

"I cannot tell you more. You give yourself to us for one week. You will be looked after, loved dare I say, spoiled, touched by the grace of angels, even."

"And?"

"And when the week ends, you will return to your old life, but maybe something in you will have been changed forever. Is that not a risk worth taking?"

Montana frowned.

"Maybe."

"I seek no answer from you now. It's only reasonable you should reflect on my proposal. We shall give you four weeks to reach a decision. If it is in the negative, you will never be bothered again."

"This is certainly unusual," Montana remarked. The tingle in her stomach had a familiar ring and the sticky wetness between her legs already held the germ of her future answer.

"How . . ." she ventured.

"Do you have a computer? At work or home?"

Montana could not help but smile. He knew only about the airport bars and the sex for free.

"Yes, I do."

The white-haired man pulled a thin notebook from his jacket pocket and scribbled quickly on it, before tearing the sheet of paper off and handing it to Montana.

"This is an e-mail number. When you have decided on your course of action, just send us a brief message. 'Yes' or 'No' will suffice and, if you are willing to take up our offer, the dates you could make yourself available. We will contact you later. And do not worry in the slightest about privacy. We are very discreet."

With that, he rose, adjusted the line of his suit and prepared to walk away.

Montana asked:

"Do you have a name, at least?"

"John," he answered and turned his back on her. A few steps later, he was out of the hotel bar and disappeared into the crowded lobby. Montana looked down at the numbers on the piece of paper he had left her.

Grey Monday at home. No dance classes. No airport bars or rooms. Montana had emerged from the shower. The house's heating was still on. She moved restless from room to room allowing the water to dry against her bare flesh.

Her mind was crowded by too many people.

Laptop. Boot up. A trip to the fridge for a glass of cold milk. Walt Disney screen-saver drifting across the monitor, Little Mermaid followed by Donald Duck followed by the Hunchback of Notre Dame embracing Esmeralda. Click. Automatic dial to her server. The familiar screen emerged, all its options beckoning her. The mouse sliding across the mat with the Citicorp logo.

She sat down. The cushion adhered instantly to her still humid rump. Her heart faltered. A familiar name caught her attention. She raced to call it up, not bothering to check its ID to save time. Sometimes, people come and go on the board so fast. She had no wish to be left high and dry.

Montana: ?

John: Hello, do we know each other or is it just a typing mistake?

Montana: It's Montana.

John: So I see ...

Montana: The airport hotel?

John: Must be another John, I fear. There are a fair number of us around!

Montana: I'm sorry, I thought you were someone else. Bye.

John: WAIT! Maybe we can talk anyway? Please.

Montana: OK, but I haven't got much time. Things to do, just logged on to get my mail.

John: So every word counts? (smile) I guess you are f. Where are you?

Montana: Paris, France.

John: Wow, same continent! I'm in Brussels. Almost up the road from you.

Montana: Interesting. But your name is not Belgian?

John: I realise it's not very gallant, but I'm working against the clock here, how old are you?

Montana: Twenty-six.

John: I'm a laser engineer. From Detroit, here on a three-month placement. I'm forty-four.

Montana: Married?

John: No. So what brings you onto the chat line?

Montana: This and that. But I must warn you, I'm not into cybergames and I am fully dressed.

John: (grin) So am I. Maybe I'm old-fashioned, but I've always considered onscreen sex as unfulfilling. I need reality. I need bodies.

Montana: Me, too. And neither will I do phone.

John: I understand.

Montana: Before you ask (i know you will), I'm 5 ft 1, redhead, 34d, slim, single, very curvy.

John: Enticing, to say the least. A veritable pocket Venus.

Montana: And I'm shaven below and have an intimate piercing, a small gold stud in my clit hood.

John: Will you marry me? (smile)

Montana: I'd have to know you better, but it's certainly not out of the question.

John: Wonderful. Your English is very good.

Montana: I am English. Came here a year ago for a man. But we're no longer together.

John: Miss him?

Montana: Sometimes. But I miss his cock more.

John: I see. Seeing anyone else right now?

Montana: No, I'm in an in-between state, I reckon. Situation available!

John: Do you work?

Montana: Yes. At the OECD.

John: What's that?

Montana: An international economic development organisation. I'm an administrator.

John: So what do you do in your spare time?

Montana: I read a lot, love movies, good meals. Tennis. Once a month, I go to Normandy for the weekend, I have friends there, and I ride horses.

John: English friends?

Montana: No, American. The Murphys.

John: Who are your favourite authors?

Montana: Scott Fitzgerald, John Irving, Katherine Mansfield, Anne Tyler.

John: We have a lot in common, you know?

Montana: Do we?

John: Yes, I'm an avid reader myself. Must shamefully confess I sometimes even write poetry. It's probably awful, I've never submitted it.

Montana: I like poets.

John: Do you?

Montana: But I usually sleep with lawyers. There is this French avocat who wants to marry me. He's quite rich. Usually comes down with me to the Normandy house.

John: Do you sleep with him?

Montana: Yes. But he never makes me come. It's rather antiseptic.

John: (smile) Can I ask you an intimate question?

Montana: Go ahead.

John: Tell me how you lost your virginity?

Montana: I was sixteen, there'd been a dance at school, he was the captain of the rugby team, we went behind the sheds. It hurt a lot.

John: Oh, Montana, you sound so nice. Real. Tender. If I came to Paris, would you meet me for a drink or a meal, maybe?

Montana: Why not?

John: You're kidding me?

Montana: No, not at all.

John: Have you ever met anyone through here, in the flesh I mean?

Montana: Yes, twice. Nice men both times. One from London, another from down South.

John: And?

Montana: They're still friends. We talk here.

John: That's very brave of you. You never know who's for real on these chat lines.

Montana: Well, I'm a forward sort of gal!

John: Sounds wonderful. What about next weekend? If I were to come down on a mid-afternoon train on Friday, we could meet up for a drink when you leave your office. You can choose the restaurant. Any one. My treat. What about it?

Montana: OK, that sounds good to me.

John: As soon as I log off, I'll phone my travel agent to get myself a hotel room.

Montana: No need to. I can put you up.

John: You mean?

Montana: Don't be silly. I have a spare bedroom, it's a large apartment. You can stay at my place. Then you'll be able to afford an even better restaurant for the two of us!

John: You sure? I wouldn't want to intrude.

Montana: Of course not.

John: Wouldn't it be awkward for you?

Montana: Listen, we're grownups. Whatever happens, happens. So, how well do you know Paris? Where do we meet. I can be free around six o'clock.

John: I mostly know the Latin Quarter.

Montana: I can make my way there, that's no problem.

John: There's a big cafe opposite the exit to Metro Odeon, on the corner of the Boulevard Saint Germain and the rue de Seine. I can't remember its name, though.

Montana: I'll find it.

John: This is wonderful.

Montana: Who knows?

John: Six on Friday then. It's a date?

Montana: Definitely a rendezvous.

John: I think I'll recognise you from your description. The clothed part at any rate (smile). Do you plan to wear anything specific?

Montana: I'll be carrying a book. A Penguin edition of Tender is the Night. Will that be OK?

John: Maybe I should tell you at least what I look like?

Montana: No need. You sound right and that's all that counts. I like surprises.

John: Wow. I feel as if we've been chatting here for years already. It'll be so great to meet you, Montana.

Montana: I'm very much looking forward to it to. Anyway, I have to go now. See you on Friday.

John: Will you be online again between now and then?

Montana: No. I have a lot of meetings, but don't be worry I shall be there on Friday.

John: Great.

Montana: I kiss you warmly.

John: I kiss you, too, most unchastely, you know where . . . (smile)

Montana: mmmmmm (smile) xxxxx

All she knew, and would ever know of Paris would be from films, TV, and magazines and postcards from friends on vacation there.

Montana recalled something she and Martin had said, early on, maybe it was only the second or third time she had spoken to him, nearly a year ago now. It was still lodged deep inside her head, impossible to erase, etched like diamond into her cortex. They had both been trying to understand why they kept on returning daily to the damn chat line. It was an addiction, they knew. Happiness, yes, that was it. They'd been discussing happiness.

He had asked her—or had she asked him?—if she was truly happy. Was a husband, a child, a house, a job, money, enough to carry you, sustain you through a lifetime?

He had quoted, she thought, a pop song about happiness being measured out in miles.

"But I'm content with inches," he had said. "I count every single one as a small victory."

"Not me," Montana had replied. "I want miles and miles. Or nothing."

She dressed. Again Montana. Again blonde and 5'9" small breasted (34A), eight-and-a-half stone, mother of one and investment analyst in the shares and securities department of

Citicorp (Montreal), Canada, Inc. Slipped on that naughty T-shirt with images of bondage her husband had once bought her, during a drunken moment, for their second anniversary and a pair of white Armani jeans.

She switched to the mail programme and typed out the e-mail.

> to: John address: 106562,2021@Compuserve.com
> from: Montana
> subject: Your proposal
>
> The answer is yes. Can do May 21st to May 27th. Let me know. Look forward to your response.
>
> In anticipation.
>
> Montana
>
> <Press Send>

The next day, a buff envelope marked "Strictly Private & Confidential" and bearing her real name was delivered by courier to the bank in mid-afternoon and brought in to her small office by the young girl at reception. She signed for it.

She held her breath as she opened it.

All it contained was a travel folder with a return plane ticket to New York for the days she had indicated to John and a brief note that read:

```
Montana,

Thank you for accepting.
No need to bring any luggage with you. You will
be met at JFK on arrival.
Your trust honors us.
```

In sweet anticipation too.

John

Before she could collect her thoughts, her phone rang. Somehow, she was convinced it would be John. As she picked up the receiver, she noticed how unsteady her hand was. But it was only Stephanie. She and her husband had effected a tearful reconciliation and she wanted to know the name of that wonderful Italian restaurant on Main Montana had once told her about, so that the reconciled couple might celebrate the occasion in style.

Montana slipped the travel documents inside her drawer, shredded the note, consigning its pieces to the waste bin and busied herself with the sheaf of stock market analysis printouts the Shares department had sent up one hour earlier. As she went through the motions of work with half her brain on standby, mentally she began to set up her necessary alibi, getting an undeniable thrill from this further venture into the realm of deception.

Following dinner that evening, and having tucked the child up in her cot, she negligently informed her husband that the bank wanted her to attend a symposium in Vancouver two weeks on. It was a plausible excuse, as she had previously attended two such conferences. All part and parcel of her job.

Her husband nodded his silent assent. Was it just an impression, but was he more distant and indifferent to her these past few months? After the trip, she decided, whatever happened, the time would come for important decisions to be taken.

By the time she joined him in bed, having spent some ten minutes ironing the outfit she was next planning to wear for the weekly portfolio meeting and a clean shirt for him for the following day, he was already sound asleep, his soft snore drifting across their bedroom. The peaceful sound of domesticity.

Out of habit, she switched on the baby alarm and, shedding her dressing gown, insinuated herself into the bed. Her side was still cold so she instinctively moved closer to him, but he felt her presence and, out of sheer habit, moved a few inches away, nearer to the edge to avoid sharing his warmth with her.

At the airport, she stored her small case, her alibi for the trip, in a locker and dropped the key to the bottom of her handbag. All she had in it were her passport, wallet, lipstick, birth control pills, disposable tissues, an address book she had carried for years (in which half the addresses or telephone numbers were now invalid), a chocolate bar, and peppermint sweets. Deliberately, she had avoided bringing photographs of either Vanessa or her husband. Somehow, it didn't feel right.

As the plane took off towards a bank of grey clouds she knew she was leaving Adrienne behind. For a whole week of sweet excess, she would be 100 percent Montana.

She had asked for an aisle seat. The plane was only half full.

An old lady sat by the window to her left and across her Montana watched the aircraft turn south as the hills of Montreal unfurled below.

It wouldn't be a long flight.

Montana tried to imagine what New York would be like, but the only images she could summon were of car chases, burly cops, and immense skyscrapers under assault from King Kong and Godzilla. She smiled. She knew it would be different from the movies.

She drifted into sleep and dreams.

She dredged up from the past the blurred faces of all the men she had been with, from college days to airport follies; she tried counting them but gave up when she noted that her arithmetic didn't make sense. Then she remembered images of their cocks. A surrealist landscape of members in all sizes, lengths, colors and appearance. Each one different and utterly distinctive, an orchestra of penises laid out at her command, mostly at attention, straight, drooping, hesitant, dangling, offensively aimed in her direction, crooked, forming every angle of the planet of geometry.

The familiar sensation inside her stomach began forming, and in her dream she knew the wetness between her legs had begun, that sticky feeling that augured of future pleasure and sometimes pain.

Unconsciously, she clasped her thighs together under her skirt.

The cocks faded. Now she sought to picture the faces of all the men she had spoken to on the Internet. Trying to put the semblance of features together with their voices. But she realized she didn't know the sound of their voices either. She stewed on impossibilities, strained at the leash in a vain attempt to seize the unseizable.

She sighed deeply. In her sleep. The old woman threw her a quizzical look as if she recognized that sigh, identified with its nature, as if it were a feeling she had known herself when younger. "Pretty girl," she thought in her native Quebecois and herself drifted into dreams, her eyes closing and no longer reading the magazine she had been holding in her lap.

Montana awoke. The plane was moving down the Jersey shore. The "fasten seat-belts" sign had come on and an attendant had nudged her to pull her seat back into the upright position.

Her short skirt had hitched itself up while she slept, revealing her stocking tops. Montana blushed. She only wore stockings when prowling for sex. She straightened her apparel, and tightened the seatbelt across her lap.

The plane began its accelerated descent, cutting across a mattress of clouds. The cabin pressure dropped and Montana felt her ears pop. She swallowed.

Panic. Sudden, unannounced. The voices in her head, the faces, the bodies were bursting, ready to explode outwards and pulverise her in the process. She wanted to scream, release this unbearable tension brewing inside her. Her fingers nervously gripped the handles of the seat as she tried to calm down.

It was all this thinking that hurt so damn much. Why couldn't she be like other women and be bland, normal, take things as they come, never much bothered about working out the whys and the wherefores? *I must think less. Or not think at all. Otherwise* . . . she knew that she would just . . . combust on the spot one day, unable to control the images and thoughts frantically racing through her poor brain like Formula One racing cars on a road to blissful oblivion. Spontaneous self-combustion, like in *The X-Files*. Verdict: the woman could not escape her own thoughts.

The aircraft landed on the runway with a dull thud.

Seated towards the front, she was among the first to disembark. There was a tall, uniformed, Afro-Carribean chauffeur waiting at the gate's exit, holding a notice-board bearing her name .

"I'm Montana," she confirmed.

"Follow me," the chauffeur said and turned on his heels, his crisp somber uniform a splash of darkness among the pastel tones of the terminal. She followed his brisk pace.

A pitch black stretch limousine with tinted windows was parked on the road outside in a No Parking zone, blissfully ignored by cops and traffic attendants. The warmth of the day surrounded her as she emerged into the light of JFK day. It was much warmer here than in Montreal, she noted.

He held the car door open for her and she entered the cool, air-conditioned, upholstered interior. The seat under her stretched and the shiny leather molded itself around her rump. The door slammed shut and daylight faded behind the tinted glass like the screen of her laptop in "sleep" mode.

The driver installed himself behind the wheel, still mute and quite disinterested in his female cargo. The partition that separated her from him rose and enclosed her in the passenger section. She could no longer see the chauffeur through it. The

engine came on, ever so quiet, a distant vibration, and the
limousine smoothly moved away from the curb.

Kennedy Boulevard. Van Wyck Expressway. Her nose
pressed against the tinted window, Montana squinted to read
the alien road signs trooping by on either side as the sleek car
dashed through the traffic like a knife through butter. Jamaica.
Queens Boulevard. Midtown Tunnel. New Jersey. La Guardia
Airport. A jumble of familiar names from acquired memories. A
bridge. A river. The Hudson? The Manhattan landscape like a
three-dimensional postcard. Buildings whose names she no
doubt knew but didn't recognise. Lexington. Traffic jam. Third
Avenue. The smell of pretzels and fat burgers and hot dogs
filtering through the warm afternoon air past the defenses of
the tinted glass. Park Avenue. The solemnity of an unending
street punctuated by trees. Madison. Her parade through the
canyons formed by the tall edifices like a modern fairy tale.

Still, the limousine wormed its way through alternately
narrow streets and car-infested avenues milling with people.

The panorama of steel and glass skyscrapers thinned and the
sleek, dark car finally slid to a halt in a small side street lined
with luxuriant trees. The steps of a brownstone mansion beckoned. As the driver opened the door for her, so did the doors of
the house and John appeared on the threshold, wearing the
same suit he had in Montreal, his smile just as enigmatic but
friendly, his posture upright, the profile of his nose leonine and
patrician.

The heat assailed her as she left the cocoon of the car. She
really wasn't dressed for this sort of weather. Should have
worn, brought different clothes. He greeted her.

"I'm so glad you agreed to come to us, Montana."

He extended a hand. For the first time, she noticed the brown
liver spots littering the back of his hands. He must be older than
she had thought.

He pointed the way up the steps and into the three-story
building.

"How did you find out my real name?" Montana asked him, stepping forward. "And where I worked?"

"We have ways, my dear . . ."

"But . . ."

"We have to know everything about those we invite to our festivities. We are very choosy, you see. But, my dear Adrienne, you will henceforth only be Montana and you must ask no more questions. Is that understood?"

She reluctantly agreed even though she was bursting with questions of all sorts.

They walked into a dark vestibule. The house was eerily silent, as if no one lived there.

"You must be tired from the journey. Shall we begin with a civilized drink? Coffee, tea? Something stronger?" They had entered a dimly lit salon, heavy with leather furnishings and with a thickly carpeted floor that swallowed the sound of their steps whole. John signaled an armchair to her.

"Tea will be fine," she said. "Funnily enough, coffee invariably sends me to sleep." She smiled.

"Tea it is."

He pressed a buzzer on a low glass-topped table. A maid appeared in an instant, silently striding into a room from a door at the back Montana hadn't noticed. She wore a black and white maid's uniform which fitted her trim body closely. Small, opaque black stockings (or maybe tights) and flat shoes. She was Japanese or Chinese—Montana didn't have the experience to tell—with lustrous hair reaching down to the small of her back.

"Tea for our guest and a mineral water for me."

The oriental maid nodded.

They remained silent until the drinks came a few minutes later. The plush decor and serene atmosphere of this house of mystery served to calm her nerves.

She had a choice.

"Do you take your tea with milk and sugar or, Russian-style, with lemon?" he queried.

"I prefer it with lemon. No sugar."

"Good choice," commented John. "Shows taste. I find the way the Brits have it with milk and sugar quite sickening."

He sipped at his glass of water, all the time observing Montana.

"I was wondering why you didn't want me to bring any of my clothes. A woman likes to be at her best," she finally said, breaking the heavy silence.

"There will be no need, Montana. We will see to all your needs. All we ask of you is to let your senses roam free. You are the main guest at our feast. You are also its sumptuous main dish. No harm will come to you, you have my word. You come here as a gift to our jaded palates. We shall treat you with all the care and devotion you undoubtedly deserve. In a few minutes, you will be shown to your room where you may rest a while from your journey. I urge you to meditate, purge yourself of the world you know, the life you come from, so that you face this week with the eyes of innocence."

His speech appeared well rehearsed as if he had given it many times before, and Montana wondered about the other women who had surely preceded her in this strange house.

She was determined to go through with it, whatever it entailed. If it was a chance to obtain answers, she was going to seize the opportunity. If it helped drown the voices and images of past and present in her crowded, painful mind, she would welcome it.

"There is only one small thing I should like to ask of you," John added. "In your room, you will find a laptop computer. I would like you to keep a daily journal of this week. One day at a time. In your own voice."

"I've never kept a diary," Montana protested meekly.

"I'm sure it will come easy to you," he reassured her and pressed the buzzer for the maid to show her to her room.

Day One

I will not write "Monday."

I have a feeling this is going to be a week unlike any other. I feel strange just being here. The house, the brownstone is strange. New York. I fear I'm not going to see much of NY. No Empire State Building, Greenwich Village or Central Park for me on this first visit. I'm amazed that it's actually taken me so long to visit New York. For what?

There is a quiet assurance about John that fascinates me. No doubt a man of many secrets. I wonder if he will fuck me during the course of this week. Maybe he will feel different from other men who have used me (with my full approval, of course). Then maybe he will not, and is only the organizer, the maitre de ceremonie for this intriguing charade I have let myself be drawn into.

The room I have been given is plush. Utterly silent. Windows double-glazed to keep out all exterior noise and kept firmly sealed to allow the concealed air-conditioning unit to function. My bed is wrought iron, quite regal, with silk sheets and the most wonderfully tactile material I have ever come across for covers: thick but smooth, almost velvetlike. I could touch it for hours and still derive gentle pleasure.

The walls are plain white, bedecked with vast mirrors with golden gilt edges. Wherever I turn, I see myself. Too much of myself. I look drawn. From the journey? From all the anxiety that preceded it? The lies?

The computer I am using is the latest Apple PowerBook model, small, sleek lines and user-friendly. My first instinct was to check whether it had a modem card, but the slot is empty. Anyway, I see no phone socket anywhere in the room. Or phone. Of course. Just one wardrobe with a beautiful silk kimono that I will have to use as a robe or dressing gown in the absence of other clothing. Everything in the bathroom is shiny and modern. The toothbrush left for me there designed by Philippe Starck in the curve of a spaceship.

Once I had grown accustomed to my new surroundings, I threw off my travelling clothes and took a shower. The water was blissfully warm and I lounged in it for longer than I should. My fingers were beginning to crinkle, God only knows what so much water did to the rest of my body. But now I feel cleansed. Ready. Buzzing with expectancy. While washing under the invigorating spray from the shower head, I had the distinct feeling I was being watched. Which excited me.

Also a bit scared.

I think of Vanessa's eyes, my lost child, my happy daughter whom I have momentarily and cruelly abandoned.

The oriental maid is here to inform me I am expected for dinner. She has left a small black dress for me on the bed. She waits while I try it on. The synthetic material adheres to my skin as if born to it. The hemline is indecently short and I see her smiling as she watches me tugging at it to cover a bit more of my thighs. It is low cut and exposes the onset of my modest cleavage. I have no underwear. While I was in the shower, the clothes I had come in had been removed from the room.

(later . . .)

There were twelve guests for dinner in a large, high-ceilinged room downstairs. And John and me at either end of the long rectangular polished oak table. The oriental maid and the black chauffeur were in attendance. Six men and six women. All wearing domino masks so that their features were partly concealed from me. I was introduced. They never spoke. The men were wearing dinner suits, some with ties in sober colours, others with colourful bow-ties; the women all wore black dresses, like me, but much longer, all reaching to the floor. They also displayed much glittering jewellery, pearls, gold bracelets and brooches à go go.

We ate in silence.

Whenever I would look up from my plate, I would catch several of the guests watching me closely, observing my table manners, my composure, the way I juggled knife, fork and glass. Thank God I was given etiquette lessons at school. There are some advantages to having been to a girl's school, although sewing never was a hit as far as I was concerned!

The food was delicious.

We began with plates of oversized oysters. Strong and succulent. I followed John's example and sprinkled every shell individually with pepper and squeezed a slice of lemon over the oyster where it blended with the oyster's natural juice, which I slurped up as quietly as possible, as he did, after eating the flesh. Some of the guests, mostly men, flavored their oysters with a tomato and horseradish paste. I tried it but it was too strong for me, disagreeably tickling my sinuses.

Followed by New England clam chowder. Creamy. Filling.

With every course, a new variety of wine was poured, which formed a perfect accompaniment to the dish, although I never had a chance to note the labels on the bottles the chauffeur circulated around the table.

The main course consisted of an enormous casserole of steaming crawfish which had been boiled and marinated in a bouillon of cajun spices. (John provided that information, one of the rare moments of conversation during the course of the meal, apart from the comments he sought from the guests on the quality of the food; they all replied laconically, in a variety of regional American and foreign accents I could not recognise; they kept on ignoring me apart from a surreptitious glance or a curious gaze, sizing me up like an animal in a zoo it seemed to me). The shellfish had been specially flown in from the New Orleans bayous that very morning, John told us.

They were wonderful. Meaty, tender, fragrant, the delicate spices drawing saliva perilously close to the edge of my mouth in anticipation as each fork approached my lips. (P.S. John, do you think I could make it as a restaurant critic? <smile>)

I ate so many crawfish I could not do honor to the remainder of the meal and had to decline tasting any of the cheeses sumptuously laid out across the individual wooden board I was offered.

The others completed the feast with coffee and cognac. I was brought tea, without having to ask.

I felt bloated, but warm and content.

We retired to another room, a vast wooden-floored sanctuary where I counted twelve deep armchairs arranged in a circle against the walls. John indicated that I should follow him and made his way to the center of the arrangement. The twelve diners had all settled in their chairs and John and I were now the focus of their attention.

The main light dimmed and another, a spot, increased in intensity, trapping John and I in its shining orbit. This new light blinded me and concealed the spectators from my view. I could be seen but not see them any longer.

"This is Montana," John said, melodramatically, laying a hand on my bare shoulder. "Our guest for this week."

I tried to act brave and feigned a small bow, while attempting a smile.

His hand descended and caught the hem of my dress and pulled it up all the way to my waist, revealing in one moment both cunt and arse. I felt my face growing warm, colors racing up to obliterate my customary pallor at being exhibited like this. But I said nothing.

A minute passed.

"Raise your arms, Montana."

I obeyed.

John moved behind me and took hold of the small black dress's two thin straps and pulled the garment over my head, which left me on complete display, utterly nude in front of this mute audience. Not once did John actually make contact with me, touch my skin, although deep inside my stomach I was aching for him to do so, touch me, manipulate me, even in front of others. I felt wanton, shameless.

The silence extended in all direction.

As I stood there, I could feel the wetness between my cunt lips increase to uncomfortable level and my nipples begin to harden.

At last, John spoke again.

"They like you, Montana. They do."

Before I could comment, words moving ever so slowly from my brain to my mouth, he continued: "That's enough for today. We will commence the ritual tomorrow. Sleep well, Montana."

He moved away, leaving me trapped alone in the circle of light. I felt a gentle tap on my shoulder. It was the chauffeur, indicating with a nod of his head I should now follow him. Shocked by his presence, my immediate reaction was to bring my hands to my breasts and crotch to *shield them from his view, but I knew the others were still watching me, testing me maybe, and I refrained from doing so. Stark naked, I followed him out of the room, deliberately walking tall. We reached the stairs leading to my bedroom and I moved ahead of him, wilfully displaying my swaying rump and maybe more to the black man's gaze.*

Before I began to write this, clad in the sheerest silk nightgown I have ever worn (found waiting for me, carefully folded, on the bed), I checked the door. It is locked from the outside.

Day Two

Only the second day, but already I am unsure whether I will be able to endure a whole week of this. So quickly, it has all spun out of control and ventured beyond even my wildest imagination. My whole body is on fire, and while my mind is advising me to cease the adventure now (but how?), my flesh is already anticipating tomorrow and my hands tremble as I bring them to keyboard for my tale.

I was woken in the morning—how early was it? My watch is no longer where I had left it on the bedside table and steel shutters seal the view from my bedroom window—by the oriental maid who brought me my breakfast on a porcelain tray. It was a frugal meal, especially after the previous evening's gastronomic delights: a glass of orange juice and a croissant. She walked back to the wall and watched me eat. Then, when I had finished, which did not take long, she asked me to follow her out of the bedroom, which I did, still clad in the sensual fabric of the nightie. We moved down a corridor to another room on the same floor of the house.

It was a smaller room, smelling of scent and spices; a coal fire roared at one end, a massive fan at the center of the ceiling swirled around, teasing the flames of the open fire and stirring the warmth through the air. One whole wall was mirrored, like a cinema screen and I sensed it was a two-way device and that I was being attentively watched on the other side of it by the diners of yesterday.

A sunken bath took up most of the room, like a jacuzzi, but without the distinctive bubbles, big enough for at least a half dozen people.

"My name is Mayee," said the maid. " I have been asked to clean and prepare you." She slipped the nightgown from my shoulders and indicated I should enter the water. As I did so, she shed her own black and white outfit. Today she was wearing no stockings, and joined me in nudity. For a brief moment, my breath halted. She was striking. Never had I seen skin so pale, features so delicate or such elegance in nakedness. This was a woman born to pose nude. Like me, she had small breasts but they conjugated perfectly with her slight body, dark brown nipples pointing upwards, washboard stomach, boyish arse, thin but perfectly formed legs. But what caught my immediate attention were her adornments. Her nipples were pierced with golden rings and her depilated pudenda was awash with fine jewellery. Minute studs, the sort other women would sport in their ears or sometimes their nose, punctured her outer sex lips on either side from top to bottom and each pair of studs connected to each other with the most minuscule gold chain, utterly denying any form of entrance to her cunt, like a chastity belt made of thin gold chain link. She joined me in the warm water and using a sponge began soaping me all over. I stood as she demanded.

Her touch was most sensual and she lingered just that extra nerve-tingling moment as she rubbed the soap over and across each erogenous zone in turn, exploring me, determining the precise location of all my soft spots. The lingering warmth of the water was soon matched by the temperature of my body.

She washed the soap away, her body moving closer to mine, skin occasionally making contact with skin before retreating again. Like a game. A series of small electric shocks. Teasing me. Firing me up. I have never had sexual relations with a woman before, but Mayee made me hungry for such a new, alien experience as she flitted across me with the towels, now raising herself out of the sunken bath and squatting on its edge to dry my shoulders and face, her vaginal piercings and fascinating chains just a few inches from my eyes, and mouth. I could smell her very intimacy and longed to be able to touch her there, feel those thin threads of gold between my fingers, my imagination *already running riot at the idea of manipulating them, pulling gently at them to observe how her sex lips would distend in reaction. But I also sensed this would not be allowed.*

The bath water drained away, gurgling as it did. But the coal fire kept my exposed body warm. She asked me to stay standing in the bath and positioned herself above me. Then she washed my hair. The smell of the shampoo was familiar, expensive, but my main memory is the feel of her fingers digging through my hair and tracing patterns of cleansing across my scalp, teasing its enhanced sensitivity.

Mayee dried my hair. Combed it.

I was then ordered to raise myself onto the edge of the bath as she descended back in, holding a small pot of white, foamy cream and a small leather box.

"Open your thighs as wide as you can," Mayee asked.

And she shaved me.

Every one of my dark blonde pubic curls was cleanly scraped away. She operated with expertise, I almost felt nothing as the sharp blade blew over me like a soft wind. First she took care of the forest above my cunt, and then, her face moving closer to my crotch, she shaved on either side my cunt lips, tugging firmly on them to increase the taut- ness and facilitate the blade's work. She rinsed me and then forced a hand between my opened thighs, under my arse, and delicately forced me to raise my pelvis and scraped away the rare wisps that lingered beneath my cunt, in the darker valley that led to my arsehole.

It felt pleasant while she cleansed me there, very sexual, but all the time my mind was working in overtime, wondering how I would ever explain this new, childlike, doll-like appearance of my pubis on my return to Montreal.

Finally, to complete her work, she sprinkled the newly shaved areas with talcum powder which she rubbed in, increasing my excitement even further. Wetness was beginning to seep out of me.

We walked nearer to the fireplace, where she anointed me with strong, heady perfumes which she liberally massaged into every square inch of my skin. Exotic, heavy, musky scents, none of which I could recognize from past shopping trips to the perfumery counters of department stores. Every fragrance seemingly selected for a different part of my body.

Finally, she had me lay down on the thick, furry carpet by the glowing fireplace and, as I watched, ground up in an earthen bowl with a pumice stone, what looked like lipstick and more talcum powder until she thus obtained a thick reddish-pink cream with which she proceeded to rouge my nipples; and, parting my cunt lips with her fingers (which almost made me climax on the very spot), coloured my outer labia scarlet. I was now a painted doll.

Ready to be played with?

Thus adorned and cleansed, I was escorted back to my room.

"Do not touch yourself," Mayee ordered as she left me there, and made her way out, her white body shining with a thin layer of perspiration from her work on me, her artistry. The door closed.

I waited.

A long time. I reckon it was late afternoon before they came for me, and my mind was already in a frenzy.

The Black chauffeur opened the door and, with a nod of his chin, beckoned me to follow him. We proceeded downstairs to the dining room. The table was set again, the twelve diners and John waiting for my arrival. I was ushered to my seat at the top of the table.

"Shall we eat?" John said.

I felt so self-conscious, now being made to eat dinner quite naked, and decorated, painted as I were. But I knew it was a test and I said nothing.

Again, the food was fantastic. Lobster bisque, laced with brandy.

Venison. Sharp, pungent, its strong taste evocative of sex and dark nights.

And I was the dessert.

Mayee and the chauffeur had cleared the dirty dishes from our main course, and emptied the center of the long, rectangular table of empty bottles and decorative flowers and candles.

"Montana, would you stand up?" John asked me.

As I did so, the chair I was sitting in was pulled away and the chauffeur took hold of me and raised me up. My mind went dizzy for a *short moment, the wine, the sudden upwards motion, but he quickly deposited me into the space that had been freed at the very center of the table. I was laid out of my back, and other hands took hold of my own hands and legs, gently pulling on them until I was quite spread-eagled across the dark, polished wood. Restraints were then attached to me so that I could no longer move.*

From his top of the table, John smiled, looking down straight into me, wide open, exposed, my sticky lips separating to offer a panoramic view of my inner pinkness.

"Shall we proceed?" he suggested.

The twelve diners rose. John was the only one to stay in his chair throughout and restricted to watch the spectacle (?). Each guest in turn selected a single dessert item of their choice and placed it over, across or in me, as I lay there defenseless. A slice of grapefruit in the hollow of my neck, a dab of rich cream to cover one nipple, a rivulet of cognac in the depression of my navel, half of a peeled banana forced delicately between my lips, a dollop of some thick, jellylike jam across my forehead forcing me to remain absolutely still, a spoonful of crème brûlée was slowly poured over my remaining nipple, a large straw-berry carefully inserted into my cunt, half in, half held by my painted labia, and on and on.

Then, each in turn, the diners came to me and ate their food off my body, never once touching me with their hands, just the grazing of lips, the soft moistness of tongues, the warm shock of mouths, the sharp contact of teeth. They all ate with indolent slowness, lingering over every bite or chew, lapping me, licking me, tasting me as they did the fruit, cream or alcohol they had selected to blend in with me.

I don't think the whole ritual lasted more than twenty minutes but I came twice.

Once the food had been consumed, my restraints were loosened and Mayee wiped me clean with a cold, wet towel.

I was helped off the table and, again, the Black chauffeur escorted me to the bedroom. Tonight, there is not even a nightgown or the silk kimono in the wardrobe. I am to be kept naked until this all ends. I must conclude this now, I have only been given half an hour to write today's entry. Any minute now, he is coming to handcuff me to the bed for the night. John said it might be too tempting to touch myself at night from now on.

He is right.

Day Three

A night without dreams.

I was a bit apprehensive about the cuffs at night, but they didn't hurt. They are lined. They think of everything.

How to describe the past day?

John, I recall, mentioned rituals. Today was the ritual of mouths.

I'm sure it was late morning already before I came awake. I'm losing perspective of time. Night. Day. Beginning to blur. All through my sleep, I had been falling, breathless, embarked on a roller-coaster ride, a big dipper whose final destination is still nowhere in sight. All my senses are alive like never before.

Mayee, in uniform again, woke me, mopping my brow after another sleep full of emptiness, as devoid of dreams (of guilt?) as a night without stars. Orange juice. Croissant. Escorted me to the bathroom and its lone designer toothbrush and tube of dental paste.

Took a pee and had a shit. She just stood there, impassive, without a shadow of a smile, watching me as I sat on the toilet. Who cares? I no longer have any shame about this utter lack of privacy. I am theirs, my body an object for their attention and observation.

The walk down the corridor to the room with the long mirror and the sunken bathtub. The eerie silence of the house. Why New York? We could be anywhere.

She bathed me, soaped me, rinsed me, dried me, then again anointed me with perfumes and rouged my nipples dark red. Yesterday's color had barely faded. Will my breasts stay permanently tainted from this week, small targets, like new hearts marked out for the executioner's firing squad?

I was expecting her to decorate my cunt lips likewise, but she did not. Instead, she adorned my painted nipples with small gold rings which she clipped on. Slightly painful at first, but my mind soon wandered away from the pain as my juices began to flow and my physical feelings concentrated on other areas of my body. I'm relieved they haven't pierced me. Like her. Would have been hell to explain at home. My now hairless sex will be enough of a problem. But I like it this way. Feels fuller, plumper; so, so pink.

A new room, circular, high ceilings, outer circle in semidarkness (but they are there, waiting, I can hear their breath, smell them), at its apex, bathed in a strong spot of white light a dentist's chair, black, sinister in appearance.

I am led to the chair. Its leather feels slippery against my bare flesh. The chauffeur (will I ever be told his name?) corrects my position in the seat. Walks to the far extremity of the chair and takes hold of both my legs, widens their angle until the muscles strain with resistance and slips them into stirrups. He moves back, and lowers the top part of the chair so that my head leans back and I can no longer embrace with my eyes the totality of my body. Another adjustment to the chair pushes my pelvis upwards eight inches or so. He moves round and, verifying my angle of vision, tilts a couple of small mirrors which appear to be floating above the chair, above my head. I now cannot avoid them. All I now see is the reflection of my own face: apprehensive, thin upper-lip, full crescent of the meatier lower lip, and in the other mirror a vision of my gaping cunt, magnified so that it occupies the whole perimeter of what I now recognise as a car's rearview mirror transplanted to this torture chair. I hear him move away.

My body could not voluntarily adopt such an obscene pose. Head back, chest and crotch thrust upwards in a parody of Aztec sacrifice and legs torn apart for a gynaecological display of my innards, which I cannot escape in the mirror that confronts me in such an adversarial but inescapable position.

There is a flutter of movement and sound beyond my field of vision.

I feel a mouth make contact with my splayed cunt lips. In the mirror, the top of a man's head, dark tousled curly hair, obscures the image of my exposed vulva.

Like an electric shock. A tremor courses through my body and the man's tongue delves slowly past outer and inner labia and grazes my clit. I hear the blood rush through my temples, feel my clamped nipples expand and my cunt lips engorge with the onset of pleasure. I also see my own face redden in the smaller mirror, my pupils dilate.

The man goes to work on me.

As his tongue explores my inner cavity, at first shying away from the more excitable zones, he slips a finger in me, long, thin. I coat it with my freely flowing juices. Having mapped the territory, his tongue soon delves further and flicks against my rising clitoris. I squirm, my perspiration already forming a wet stream between my skin and the black leather of the dentist's chair. All the time, I watch the expression on my face, as pleasure gets the better of me and my senses shed all inhibitions.

The man knows what he is doing. He teases me awfully, with tongue and finger, each time slowing down or retreating whenever my body betrays my excitement. I see and feel his head move back and the finger rising through the opening of my cunt and I watch with outraged fascination as it reaches my clitoral hood and, joined by another marauding digit, pinches my clitoris, now so engorged it appears in the magnifying glass like a small, deformed penis.

Below, his tongue plunges into me again, brushing against my inner walls. His two fingers persist in cruelly handling my clit, squeezing, pulling, plucking it, micro-massaging it. I gasp. A visible tremor moves across my stretched belly. His fingers move away, to be replaced by his mouth and my clit is now held between his teeth and being licked mercilessly by his tongue. Then he chews on it, with utter languor and detachment, refusing to match course with the torrential waves of pleasure making their way through me. I try to hold back, to wait until I can marry the lust wave roaring inside with his movements in and against me, but I succumb and I come. I scream, as I do so. Probably invoking Jesus. I know I always do, can't help it, it's what a Catholic upbringing does for you!

Having provoked my orgasm, the man moves back from my open thighs. Mayee mops my brow (I recognise her hands).

I've barely had time to breath when another mouth invades me. In the mirror, I see it is a woman from her long auburn hair trailing all the way down her back. My face reddens intensely. I have never had sex with a woman before. Her touch is different, not as rough, more teasing. She refrains from using her fingers and concentrates mostly on the nub of my clitoris. Her caress is so slow I feel like bellowing my lungs out and begging her to make me come faster. But she expertly rides my pleasure, unhurried, systematic, tender. My face in the mirror is obscene, contorted, painted with unbearable vulgarity as lust controls me. I come again. My whole body leaps in the chair, straining against the ties that bind me to it (my hands were at the onset immobilised against the metal sides of the chair).

Mayee wipes away the perspiration from my face.

Another mouth. A man, balding. He hasn't shaved for a few days, his rough skin tears against my depilated pubis (when he retreats later and I get an unencumbered view of my splayed cunt captive in the screen of the rearview mirror, it is all red, like an open wound). But his ministrations are delicate, he plays with my cunt like an orchestra and takes me to another, almost serene, level of pleasure and I orgasm again.

Another woman follows him. Blonde. Her lips are dry. My mind has by now lost all control and thereafter I no longer even remember the sequence of events. My consciousness just blacked out. I became a body reduced to cunt. And eyes. Avid voyeur of the spectacle of lust disfiguring me on and on and on again. With some, I would come at first touch, with the mere flick of a tongue against clitoris or lips against labia. Others made the agony last longer, until time stopped existing. I floated in a perpetual state of high arousal, an animal of sex. The juices were dribbling like a stream from my gaping cunt, mingling with the saliva of my cunnilinguists and my own, abundant sweat. This river pooled between my thighs, sliding down between my arse crack, and my whole body squelched against the chair's leather as every new orgasmic wave raced through me, like the deadly current through the body of a criminal on the electric chair.

I know there were twelve. Maybe some had me more than once. I lost count and soon I could no longer make out the difference between man and woman; my eyes could no longer focus on the images of their heads, down there, eating me, to distinguish their gender. I invoked Jesus in vain often enough to court eternal damnation, and no doubt proffered even worse obscenities and guttural noises as pleasure reduced me to Neanderthal level. I begged for more, I wanted more, and as soon as one orgasm reached a plateau my body screamed out for the next. At one stage, I even peed myself. I was no longer in control of any of my functions. My oral lover sensed it coming and safely retreated, allowing me a full view in that damn mirror of the river of urine spurting from my depths in an impossible arc. But I was no longer capable of shame.

Somehow, it came to an end. All I remember is my hands and feet being unshackled. The room appeared empty now, with the exception of Mayee, the chauffeur and me. I was helped out of the chair and my legs buckled, I had to be supported all the way upstairs.

My body was alight and still screaming inside for more. I was, even after several hours of repeated orgasms, still unfulfilled.

Mayee towelled me down in the bedroom. She could read my uncensored thoughts (was it so obvious?).

"You still need cock, don't you, Montana?" she said, with a wry smile.

I blushed (could I get any redder in the face?) and nodded.

The chauffeur had been standing by the door, holder of the keys. She summoned him over.

"Everything in its time, Montana," Mayee said. "Just a little something to keep your appetite in check."

My juices were still dripping down my thighs. The black man loosened his trousers, I lowered myself to my knees. He was enormous, sleek, ebony, thick, at least ten inches, and I took him inside my mouth, sucking greedily until his glans hit the back of my throat. He was as hard as solid wood and I feasted myself on him, like a baby at his mother's teat. He came, copiously. He tasted strong and bitter.

"Enough," concluded Mayee and my day reached its end.

Day Four
As soon as my eyes opened, my body came alive. Every nerve hypersensitized, aching, throbbing with pain and desire. They hadn't

cuffed me to the bed the night before. There had been no need. I was so spent that the idea of pleasuring myself was the last thing on my mind.

Then the same routine I have grown accustomed to. Breakfast. Brushing teeth and toilet duties under Mayee's watchful gaze. The bath. So warm and inviting I could spend an hour more in it, but her vigorous scouring of my skin soon returned my sharpened senses to the reality of the world of pleasure.

Today she added a teaspoonful of fine gold leaf to the red paste she applies to my sexual parts. I now glow, the mouth of my cunt like a vagina dentata, sparkles with gold amongst its rawness.

The corridor. The other room. The dentist's chair. I am positioned into it by the strong black arms of the chauffeur. I notice the seat has been cleaned of my previous day's abundant secretions. The angle between my legs is widened and I feel myself come open immediately. I know I am already fully engorged and the view they have of me is positively pornographic. My ankles slip into the stirrups and are fastened. I voluntarily let my hands drift down to my sides, where they are taken and bound. He operates the chair's mechanism and my torso and pelvis are thrust upwards to accentuate my angle of display and the section supporting my head is lowered back. I see there are no mirrors gerrymandered above me. Today, I will not bear witness to the ravages of lust aging my features in their ugly rictus.

Yesterday's scenario is being modified.

I don't even contemplate the implications. My brain lies dormant. I am just body. Cunt.

I hear something being dragged across the floor and positioned behind me, below the level of my head support.

John approaches. Wordless.

He holds a small flask and, watching me attentively, pours some of its silky yellow liquid into the palm of his hand and massages the oil into my breasts, concentrating on the nipples and aureolae, rubbing deep, and then doing likewise, oiling my bare pubis, deeply massaging the plump flesh of me.

As soon as his hand retires, I feel the skin he has oiled sting atrociously. I clench my teeth and allow the pain to spread. Within a minute I am on fire. My sexual parts shriek with the despair of longing. I need. I want. I demand. The burn has to be appeased.

I don't have long to wait.

John retreats and a man—naked, domino-masked, cock erect, hairless chest—places himself between my legs, he extends his hand and parts me, positions his cockhead on the cusp of my inflamed lips and impales me in one swift forward motion.

"Jesus almighty!" I can't help screaming.

He fills me more with every thrust, grows bigger within, his heavy balls slap against me as his rhythm accelerates. He is like a machine, ploughing into me, relentless. A storm of senses dances wildly inside my body as the first man fucks me. I already sense that there will be others.

Then, sounds of steps behind me, another man raises himself on the stall that had been placed there and lowers his half tumescent member towards my mouth. I take him and begin licking and sucking him to hardness as the first man comes and goes between my thighs like an unholy piston. I am now a forest fire, all-consuming, consumed, devoured from within and outside. The air making its way into my lungs feels thin and my stomach has turned to jelly.

The pattern has been established. As one takes me, I suck the next to full erection, suitably lubricating his cock with my saliva before he takes over from his spent predecessor and enters me. I am an automaton. A sex machine. Giving with my mouth, taking with my hungry cunt.

Some come inside me, I recognise the tremor in their bodies, the tremulous shaking motion of their cocks buried deep within me and the sudden spurt of warmth; others disengage and ejaculate over my stomach, sometimes even reaching as far as my breasts, coating me with their emissions, their essence. On and on it goes. And all the time, I know the others are watching, enjoying with glee the spectacle of my ravishing, their eyes fixed like magnets on the vision of alien cocks stretching me to all heaven, ferociously drilling into me. Some men come in silence, others moan, others groan, one even shouts, "Oh,

God!". He was red-haired and very thick and dug his nails deep into my raised arse as he fucked me.

The chair rocks. I leek copiously. Sweat beads down my forehead, moves down and settles in the form of a small lake in the valley between my shaking breasts, then overflows and streams farther downwards, past of the dam of my cunt and its attendant embedded cock, on to the black leather of the chair between my anal crack, where it is joined by the canal of come and cunt juices and spreads in concentric motion under my body. I am swimming. I am floating.

I come. I come. I come.

I wriggle as I am speared. I beg for mercy. I growl for more punishment. I live for cock.

The parade goes on for hours. My hearing now sharpened like a knife, I hear the six women in the audience pleasuring themselves: little gasps, deep breaths emerging from the darkness of the room, as they bear witness to my hardcore movie.

This goes on for what seems like forever. I soon lose count. But there were more than six of them, I am positive. Or maybe all of them fucked me at least twice or three times. After a while, the differences between their ramming members battering away at the apex of my legs begins to blur. I welcomed their incessant invasion, I craved for further humiliation, because every stroke of a thick cock inside me, every pink or purple glans pushing its way past my lips, gifted me with yet another degree of undescribable pleasure.

I wanted it all to go on forever. Until I was torn beyond repair, bled from every orifice. Died.

This is how it felt. This is who I am.

May whoever reads this know what an abject creature I am.

Day Five

Who are these people, the twelve and John? What are they in real life? Do they have families, children?

Words again fail me after a further day here. I am tired. Awfully scared of the days in New York still to come. Something John whispered in my ear before I was shown to my bedroom again. What happens on the seventh day. Am I disposed of like a soiled rag? My imagination is as inflamed as my body and speculates wildly about my eventual fate.

How can words even approach to explain the feelings, the events?

Today, the dining room was littered with comfortable rugs and animal skins, the massive oak table transported elsewhere. Blinding bright light illuminating every corner of the room. A stool with a cushion. I am made to lower my stomach on to it, raising my rump upwards as my feet get a feeble grip on the floor. This time Mayee rubs the strong, piercing, sense-arousing oil into my parts, breasts, cunt and today my anal aperture, her nail entering me partly: scratching, burning. She is still daubing me when the fire takes hold, inner furnace and sexual yearning leaping from my body like tongues of flame, seeking relief in touch and penetration.

I don't have to wait long. My legs are roughly kicked apart and my rear is splayed open for all to contemplate. A cock, soft and hard, silky and warm, positions itself at opening of my anal sphincter and applies quiet but steady pressure. I begin moaning in protest at this new intrusion, but a hand gags me momentarily. Out of the blue, the man standing between my legs violently smacks both my arse cheeks, repeatedly, painfully. I jump. The women on either side of me take hold of my hands and immobilize me in their grasp.

The man pushes again. Merciless. I feel as if I'm being split apart. The sphincter gives up its resistance and his glans enters me. It feels like a large cork plugging me. He stills himself for a moment, my arsehole partly breached, and as he slaps me again gives an almighty push forward and buries his whole cock inside my arse. I want to scream. I cannot endure this pain any longer, but my cries are muffled and my body adjusts to this new invasion, the waves of pleasure rise and gradually submerge the pain.

Another cock is placed in my mouth and the come and go in my bowels begins in earnest. Every thrust goes further than the one before, the reef of decency assaulted over and over again. I am sucking so hard on the cock inside my mouth that the man comes quickly. I barely taste his frothing ejaculate before it slides down my throat as my mouth, full to the brim, gasps for air. And still the other sodomises me wildly, 'il m'encule', forever stretching these new boundaries to my body. The pain is intense, but so is the joy. With one final savage thrust that echoes throughout my body, he comes noisily in my bowels. I feel the added moistness of the invasion. He pulls out as suddenly as he had earlier entered me. More pain radiates through me in reaction to the brutality of his withdrawal and another man takes his place and enters my dark, gaping orifice. The first man moves to my front, holding his fast detumescing member in one hand and presents it to my mouth. It smells strongly of me, of him, of lust, of shit, of us. He pushes the glistening cock coated with the fruits of our desire into my mouth and I taste a part of myself I had never tasted before.

They all take turns despoiling me. Between cocks, I feel the monstrous dilation of my arsehole as the ambient air caresses its dripping opening, its ridge covered with come and faecal matter. The hole has become so large that I fear it will never close again.

I am helped from my prone position, angled over the stool and led to a rug. Around me all twelve are naked, men and women. Bodies in all varieties and shapes and ages.

A blonde woman whispers sweet nothings in my ear as she helps me lay down and puts her mouth to my lips and kisses me. I open my lips and allow her tongue to enter me. Hands caress my breasts. Lips slide over my cunt and another mouth begins licking away the juices and matter surrounding my despoiled anal overture. Soon, a woman's cunt offers itself to me, and for the first time I taste a woman in her intimacy. A cock slipped into me as I lay sideways. A hand lovingly tousles my hair.

I close down my sanity and allow myself to float away on the blissful waves of desire.

Two men inside me, one in cunt, one in arse, their respective cocks teasing each other across the thin membrane separating both openings. My mouth avidly holding another cock, then chewing on a woman's odorous, parted vulva.

My tongue delving deep into the dark stained star of a man's rear hole as a woman eats me with furious appetite.

My lips taste the spicy tongue of a redhead while another man fucks her, then moving downwards across the sensuous animal pelt to watch how his cock has buried itself in her depths in unimaginable close-up, his balls hang, hairy, I lick them as he thrusts in and out of her.

I watch another man take a hard cock in his mouth before he is in turn mounted, noticing as he is taken that the cock now buggering him leaps outwards from a metal cock ring. I don't recall feeling it against me in earlier trysts.

A man fucks another man who fucks me in the arse as I paw at another woman's breasts.

Four sets of hands take a hold of me and splay me utterly, holding my extremities as far away from my body as human anatomy permits, whilst two men maneuver themselves and enter my cunt simultaneously. I ache. But my muscles give in and they fill me.

I drink of their come and juices as they feast on me.

Every unholy combination is attempted and succeeds, with me at its apex, center and heart.

Cries. Moans. Groans. Sighs. Tears.

I am used and will never be the same as before.

Darkness, I sense, has fallen outside the house.

We have been copulating in the final circle of hell all day. I am exhausted. Mindless. I am sex incarnate.

Once again, I am led up the stairs, the Black chauffeur holding me under the shoulders as I stumble over the steps.

"That was very good, Montana. Very good indeed. You are gifted. I knew you would be from the first time I saw you."

It's John, standing at the top of the stairs. He was not present earlier while I was being defiled and shaming myself totally. Beast of lust, no longer woman.

I move past him, still in a state of shock, eager for the quietness of the bedroom.

He whispers: "Tomorrow."

I look back, and through my dry lips, does he even hear me, ask: "What?"

"Tomorrow the dogs, maybe . . ."

I am scared. How further can I go, can my body endure any more of this sensual folly until it just gives up on me? What more can they do to me?

There is a platter of fresh fruit waiting for me on the bedside table. I am ravenous.

Will I cry all night or will I sleep?

The solemn quietness of morning settled. Montana opened her eyes.

Every nerve end in her body was being sharpened, scraped by sandpaper. Every tendon, bone, and ligament buried deep below her skin ached in unison. A muted form of pain radiated outwards from her sexual parts. And fear, like a malevolent cloak, surrounded her.

She squinted against the invading sunlight. The steel shutters barricading the windows had been opened. She looked around apprehensively. No breakfast tray. No Mayee to shake the torpor of sleep out of her. The silence of the house was heavier than before.

She rose from the light cocoon of the silk sheets and looked around her. The clothes she had travelled to New York in were carefully draped across a chair. Meticulously ironed.

She turned in the bed, searching for the small table. The computer was no longer there.

Montana rose from the warm bed and seized the envelope now sitting where the laptop had been. Opened it.

Her Pierre Cardin watch, a honeymoon duty-free gift. Showing 10:30 A.M. An airline ticket. JFK to Montreal. Departing at 4 P.M. And a green hundred dollar bill clipped to a torn piece of yellow legal paper. With the message:

This should cover your cab to Kennedy. Try and get there at least one hour before the flight's departure. I apologize for my cruel joke. It was tasteless. Sometimes I can be overtly facetious. I'm sorry. I hope you will not think the worse of me. Thank you for everything. You were great. John.

❐

Montana washed her face, dressed and ran down the familiar corridor and stairs. As she now expected, the brownstone was quite empty. They had all departed. Each room at peace, with not the slightest indication anywhere of the acts which had so recently taken place here. The oak dinner table stood squarely in the formal dining-room. The sunken bath was empty. After some exploring, she even found the dentist's chair, stored away in a broom cupboard. It now looked so innocuous. Normal.

Clutching her handbag, she turned the door handle and the hundred noises and odors of the New York streets assaulted her. The sound of children playing and birds. The smell of a late spring day. A small, tree-lined street. A yellow cab cruised by. Montana hailed it.

Misfits of Eros

A taxi carried her quickly from airport to home. The rush hour had subsided and the traffic had been light. She slotted her key into the door and opened it.

Dropped her case of unworn clothes to the floor in the entrance hall.

Her husband was sitting , morose, at the kitchen table, with the remains of his evening meal, a tomato and cheese omelette, still lingering on his plate. And a half-full bottle of wine and a single glass. Montana approached him and kissed his forehead.

"You never even phoned," he said, visibly unhappy.

"I know," she answered. "The way things go. Busy. Never free at the right time to call. How's Vanessa?"

"She just fell asleep a short while ago. Try not to wake her when you go to her room. She's been very irritable all week, with you away. You could at least have tried to phone," he went on.

"I'm sorry. I really am."

She took a clean glass from the cabinet and helped herself to some wine, although she'd never really liked the taste of red wine, a traitor to the French blood in her veins from a couple of generations back.

She sipped it slowly, gazing at her husband's features, trying to guess whether he was genuinely suspicious or just his surly, uncommunicative self. The latter, she concluded.

"I'm very tired. I really have to sleep. Long journey," she said.

He nodded.

She moved to their bedroom.

Montreal, a city dominated by two hills. One French, one

English. Two cultures. Montana was a product of both, with a mother from Quebec and a father from Ontario. This was her city, the place where she had been born and brought up, but now it seemed alien to her. Provincial. A straightjacket for her bubbling emotions. She reintegrated reality, took small comforts from the twinkle in her daughter's eyes, the sight of her growing, gleefully trying out new words, gliding through the world of innocence like the sweet child she was; she accepted the kindness of her husband's predictable embraces and took refuge in her work at the bank. The only job she had ever held, straight from her degree in economics at the university. Spreadsheets and stock market movements did not lie, required no heart to decipher their secret language. Facts. Figures. She was determined not to return to her old world, to the mindless angst of Mondays trawling the airport bars and teasing unknown men on the Net.

She had seen the other side of life and what she had learned there was deeply unpleasant. She had come face to face with her real nature and the stark, ugly vision was now a scar within her she would never be able to fully erase. Another burden to endure on the long nights lying awake in bed.

It wasn't until three days after her return from New York that her husband, shaving by the sink, noticed her bare pubis as she emerged dripping from the shower one morning.

"What the hell is that?" he exclaimed, his lathered face comically registering his surprise.

"In Vancouver," she answered. "I think there must have been some fleas or something in the bed at the damn hotel. It was itching so much beneath my curls, I just got quite paranoiac and shaved the lot away."

She knew she didn't sound convincing, but she couldn't come up with anything better.

"Let me see," her husband said and took a closer look at her depilated pudenda.

Montana held her breath, ready for further questions she

would have no answer to. At least, there were no visible marks from her New York activities across the rest of her body. Her many lovers had been very careful in that respect. Even her apertures were no longer so red and raw.

"It's growing back a little already," her husband said.

He peered down at his wife's sex.

"A bit like my chin when I haven't shaved for a couple of days," he smiled.

Encouraged by his response, Montana asked, "What do you think?"

"If you kept it that way, I wouldn't mind."

"Wouldn't you?"

"No. I must confess I find it very sexy. Arousing. I never told you, but when they shaved you there for the baby's birth, I was so turned on. But for a few weeks we couldn't do much about it, remember and it had already begun growing back."

"You never told me," Montana said.

"Keep it that way, my love," he asked her. "I'd like that."

Her face brightened. Out of relief, and by her husband's sexual revelation. She took a step back and sat herself on the edge of the bath and opened her legs wider.

"In that case, while you have the lather and razor at hand, you might as well begin the upkeep of your new toy."

He laughed and moved towards her. For the first time in years, they made love before breakfast that morning while Vanessa conveniently lingered in her room playing with her dolls. Both were late for work.

As he hurriedly knotted his tie in front of the bedroom dressing table mirror, he asked Montana:

"Have you given any thought to our conversation of the other month?"

"Which one?" she asked, although she knew very well.

"About having another child," he said.

"I'm still thinking, love. It would be such a big step to take, you know."

"I know, I know," he said, slipping his suit jacket on. "But it would be nice."

Montana, dressing on her side of the bed, slipping her long legs into today's pair of tights, felt she should say more, but before she could, the childminder called out from Vanessa's room that the child expected a final kiss from her mummy, once again leaving the subject open, like a sword held above her mind. A decision she must soon take if she didn't want her marriage to take a step in the wrong direction. She was unlocking her car door when she had a weird realization: she could not remember when was the last time her husband had bought her flowers!

Driving to the bank through the gridlocked traffic, Montana kept trying to visualize what a baby boy would look like, how different he would be from chubby Vanessa as a newborn. She could conjure up no precise image. Her mind was a complete blank. She reached the office and rushed into her first meeting with only seconds to spare. Her departmental boss frowned at her as she sat herself in her usual place at the conference table, still short of breath from her frantic run up the stairs and through the corridor. The agenda was passed around the table. Far East futures. Biotechnology start-ups risk investment factors. A comforting routine.

Another analyst was on pregnancy leave and Montana had agreed to forego her Mondays off for three months (on overtime pay), but the workload hadn't spread in proportion. During lunch hours, sandwiches or takeaway hamburgers and chips, she continued to log on from time to time. Curiosity, yearning? She wasn't sure.

While most of her colleagues puffed away at their stolen nicotine time in the small square that faced the bank's granite building, Montana remained in her office, door closed, and surfed the chat lines.

She listened to the song of the Internet. The lament of the lost.

Montana: And what do you come here for?

Richard: Just chat, someone to talk to. It's not easy in real life, you see. How do you start a conversation with a total stranger. Easier here. Don't you find it so?

Montana: I work in a bank in Calgary.

Alice: You're so lucky to be in a big city. I'm stuck in this small town, two hours drive north of Seattle. Since he left me, I've put on so much weight. No man would want me now. But there is this man in Germany. He should be calling me here any minute now.

Montana: So, hopeful of romance?

Alice: No. I made a silly mistake after we had got on so well in our first talks to mail him a photo. Didn't tell him it was over ten years old (sigh).

Montana: I have a daughter. She's like a ray of sunshine in my life.

Lucy: Mine have now left home. I miss them so badly. They phone, sometimes return for the weekend, but it's not the same thing. Why did they ever have to grow up? Silly, hey? They were perfect as babies. I wish they could have stayed that way forever.

Montana: Mine is already changing, becoming her own person.

Lucy: It's the beginning of the end, you'll see.

Montana: Lonely? Well, maybe a bit.

Thomas: I am, desperately so. I can't hide the fact any longer. But I thought you were married?

Montana: So what do you do?

Ann: I hand craft jewellery.

Montana: Do you have many customers, working from home?

Ann: I get by. It's not much of a life, but it's all I've got.

Montana: That sounds interesting ...
Christian: Not really.

Montana: When did you see her last?
Joe: It's coming up to six years in August. I sound ridiculous, don't I? Sure, there have been other women since, but just the thought of her still makes my heart crack up. Every few months, I write, I beg forgiveness, but she never answers. I no longer know if she even lives at the same address. Christ, it hurts!

Montana: What did you do?
Michael: I bought her a theatre ticket and sent it anonymously. To see if it would intrigue her enough.
Montana: So?
Michael: She used it. Went to the performance. 'The Real Inspector Hound' it was.
Montana: And sat next to you? Did you speak to her?
Michael: No. I had a seat two rows back from her. All I could see was the back of her head.

Montana: And your husband found out?
Karyn: Yes. And he's never forgiven me since. Barely talks to me or touches me any more.
Montana: What are you going to do, then?
Karyn: There's nothing I can do. I have no money, no education. It's been ages since I've worked. Who'd want a forty-plus cosmetics assistant when you have so many younger and prettier ones around. I'm trapped.
Montana: Do something.
Karyn: But he's a good provider. I can't complain about that.

Between the prowlers and the frauds, the predators and the sex beasts, all she could hear was the forlorn melody of ache. I yearn. I miss. I love. I crave. I hurt. I want. I had. I lost.

◱

They took a week's holiday in northern Quebec, among the fragrant pine forests and myriad lakes. Her husband would spend the day fishing. Montana played for hours on end with the child, locking away for posterity every word, every one of Vanessa's smiles.

But there was tension when the two of them were alone together. Unspoken words. Reticence. Meals taken in silence. Unfinished gestures. The lovemaking lacked passion. She was glad to return to work the following week. All she could show off was a gentle tan.

mk: Hi! There you are. It's been ages. Where have you been?

Montana: Here and there. Everywhere. Holidays, work, business trips.

mk: I missed you so much, Montana.

Montana: You were always in my thoughts, Martin.

mk: Was I?

Montana: You were.

mk: So where does that leave us?

Montana: What do you mean?

mk: Us, Montana. You and me?

Montana: Where we always were, Martin. I like you very much.

mk: I want more.

Montana: I know. So, tell me about the tropical islands you would take me too. I do so like those stories. Once you wrote about how you would lick the salt off my body after I'd emerged from my early morning swim, remember?

mk: I do. But I just can't go on any longer like this, Montana ...

Montana: Why?

mk: It's not leading anywhere. We're racing in top gear through some loop that never ends, like a serpent chasing it's tail. It's killing me, it is. Every time I log off after talking to you, I feel so blue.

Montana: I'd rather cheer you up!

mk: Montana, this is the last time I will ask. See me. Agree to

meet. Otherwise, there's no longer any point in us talking here
again. We just say goodbye today and ignore each other when we
happen to be in the same chat room in future. Are you so damn
afraid of what might happen if we do finally meet face to face?

Montana: Yes, I am.

mk: Take that risk, my love. I'm literally on my knees.

Montana: It's not meeting you that chills my heart, Martin. It's
what I would feel like after we part, as we inevitably would. Both
to return to our respective families. I don't know if I could stand
that hurt.

mk: OK.

Montana: Don't you understand the situation from my point
of view?

mk: I try to, but it doesn't mean I have to approve it. Goodbye,
Montana.

Her heart skipped a beat. Outside her door, her departmental colleagues returning from lunch break were noisily trooping down the corridor, exchanging gossip and mindless banter.

Montana: No. WAIT!

mk: Yes?

He was married. He had two almost-grown children. He was twenty years older than she was. His words often touched her in places she didn't know she had. He could wax impossibly poetic. He had slept with other women he had met here, she knew. He could make her smile. He was wealthy, she knew. He lived so far from her, on another continent. He moved her. Was her delicious secret, untainted, clean. She longed to hear the sound of his voice.

Montana: Yes.

mk: You mean?

Montana: Come to Canada and we will meet. I agree.

mk: Oh, Montana. I can't believe it. This is wonderful and, by the way, I do accept your invitation.

Montana: (smile)

Initial arrangements were impatiently made. All afternoon, monitoring stock movements at her desk, as the markets continued their frenzied topsy-turvy rides through virtual money, Montana could feel the sheer lightness taking hold of her heart. She stayed behind after office hours, and surfed the net for all the information she could find about Toronto restaurants and streets. She hadn't been there since the age of sixteen, for the wedding of a distant cousin, and still remembered the wandering hands of an English boy exploring the lack of opulence inside her blouse at the large party held on the lawn. Half a life away, she realized.

My lovely darlings,

This is a difficult letter to write. I am going away for two or three days. I know how this will look. Bad. But it is not what it appears to be. My mind, my head are in a whirl of conflicting feelings and emotions and I badly need some time on my own to think things over. Reflect on my life and who I now am. On us. I ask your forgiveness and hope you will attempt to understand this sudden decision. I have not taken it lightly. I will probably go to Ontario, to one of my relatives but I beg you not to try and search for me there. These are days where I must remain alone with my sad thoughts, to sort out the lies from the truth. Reading the above, I reckon it will probably not make much sense to either of you, but there we go, this is it, this is me. Do believe me when I say that I will miss you both awfully and will think of you every minute of every day. That is a promise. When I return, which I will, we will start again and make things work better.

With all my love,

Adrienne

She felt a hand on her shoulder. Light. Hesitant.

"Montana?"

The voice was deep, seductive, everything she could have expected and more. It spoke of tenderness. With an accent like the quality plays on the TV.

Montana stood in the cavernous foyer of Toronto's Royal York Hotel. She was five minutes early for their appointment and had been gazing up at the tiers of balconies surrounding the main registration area, layers of plush armchairs and potted plants dotted around its periphery.

She turned round to face him, a knot slowly forming in the pit of her stomach.

"Martin?"

"Yes. It's me"

They had exchanged photos of course, scanned to jpg format for e-mail download, but there he was for real. He wasn't quite as tall as she had imagined, in fact the same height as her, not as lean either, middle-age spread already straining against the waistband of his trousers, and nowhere near as pale. His skin had a natural olive hue which gave him a very European look.

He smiled. Proffered his hand.

"At last," he said.

She shyly smiled back at him.

"You're so much better than the photograph you sent me," Martin said. "Quite beautiful, you know."

She extended her hand in turn and formally shook his, and then all the memories of their online conversations flooded back and she moved closer to him and kissed him on the cheek. The familiarity took him by surprise. He didn't return the kiss.

She looked at him again, the dark suit, the blue shirt, the open neck collar revealing early tufts of chest hair.

"Not quite what you expected?" he asked.

"Slightly different. Of course, but then photographs never tell the whole truth, do they?" she answered. "But you'll do fine.

For now . . ." She hoped she'd said it with the right touch of irony in her voice.

"You look absolutely . . ." he searched for the right word, ". . . luminous."

'What does a girl answer to that?'

"Nothing. It was a statement of fact, was not even meant as a compliment."

The hotel guests milled around them, a babel of dozens of different languages, and piles of assorted suitcases and match-ing luggage.

"You're staying here, are you?" Montana asked him.

"Yes," Martin answered. "It's a place with good memories."

"Should I ask?" she ventured.

"No. Not what you think. Shall we go and have a drink, a coffee, somewhere?" he suggested. They had been glued to the same spot for over ten minutes.

She suggested looking for Yonge Street.

They spoke for hours. Life stories, childhood, anecdotes both thought they had forgotten, of triumphs and disappointments, friends and foes, places and times. Delighted in the minute coincidences scattered amongst the revelations, despite the years and distance that had, until now, separated them.

"Am I talking too much?"

"No. Not at all. Do go on. Tell me more, and more . . ."

It was no longer a conversation that had to be contained, circumscribed over two lines at a time on a computer screen before transmitting and waiting for a tardy response. Their dialogue overlapped, repeated itself, swung in all directions as subjects changed in the same sentence and intimate confidences made way for delightful confessions. By now, both knew profoundly how right it had been to finally agree to meet and began to bitterly regret all the opportunities they had wilfully missed before.

But still things were left unsaid.

Late afternoon. Brushing of fingers over the table top.
Neither wishing to raise the matter of what came next.
He circled the subject as delicately as he could.

"What time do you have to be home? Would you like to have something to eat?" he asked, probing.

"Food would be nice," Montana said.

"My treat, then," Martin suggested.

They found an Italian trattoria some hundred yards away from the quiet coffee house they had spent the afternoon, in the shadow of a large mall that dominated the area.

The service took forever and they both consciously avoided ordering dishes with garlic.

"That was nice."

"Yes, it was."

He settled the check, pushed his coffee cup aside and took Montana's hand in his. He was so warm to touch, she noted.

"Well?"

"Well."

"I'm here for a few days. Have an open return ticket. It's been really . . . nice. Even better than I had expected, Montana."

"Yes, it has," she nodded.

"I hope you can find some spare time to see me tomorrow, maybe?"

She made up her mind. In fact she had taken the decision days ago already, and these preliminaries were just a needless excuse to delay the fateful moment. She put her hand in his.

"I'll come back to the hotel with you, Martin. If that's what you want," Montana said, enjoying the sheer warmth of his hands over the checkered tablecloth.

"You will? I didn't dare ask. Of course, I must be honest, the prospect was always at the back of my mind, how could it not be, but I was afraid to suggest it. Too scared shitless you might actually say no."

"Silly."

"What about your husband, isn't he expecting you back soon?"

"I told him I was sleeping over at a friend's place. We live away from the city center. There's no need to worry."

"So, you planned this a little, didn't you?"

"A little, but so did you, no?"

"I suppose so."

"A pity you're staying in a hotel, though. I'm not too fond of hotel rooms. Something about them," Montana said.

"What?" he asked her.

"It's a long story. Maybe one day I will tell you. It's a nice evening, shall we walk back?" She rose from her chair.

A hotel room is just like any other hotel room, reckoned Montana. Even at the upmarket Royal York in Toronto. She drew the curtains, obscuring the view of the railway station and the CNN needle.

Martin's case was on the bed, where he had thrown it earlier; not even bothering to unpack after his transatlantic flight in his haste to meet her. He must have flown in just that morning. Just for her.

"Christ, you're so beautiful, Montana," he says under his breath, but she hears every word. And yes, it sounds so nice in his warm voice.

They orbit briefly around each other, noticing how the light shines against his glasses, against her cheekbones, closely storing these early memories of each other's faces. He smells her. She feels the heat from his body radiating towards her. They kiss.

He tastes the subtle cocktail of her breath. A minty undertone, a sweetness that lingers over her muskiness.

Their tongues collide in slow motion as they probe each other, gourmet lovers who know they have all the time in the world. The universe is abolished outside the circle of their affection. The kiss lasts forever until they are both about to gasp for breath and separate. Briefly. Then tongue wraps itself around tongue again as lips meet. It's a vampiric embrace as each in turn attempts to suck the other's soul and last bubble of air out of the partner's lungs. Gasping. Hearts fluttering to the beat of a rock 'n' roll drum. Hands move slowly on bodies, gliding over material, guessing what the flesh below will feel like when clothes are later shed. The first moments of sex when every image, every thought, every gesture will stay imprinted in the mind forever.

They separate.

"Let's do this right," Montana says and pushes his suitcase off the bed, then pulling off the bedcover to reveal immaculately white sheets. She kicks her shoes off. Martin stands there watching, hypnotised by the sheer beauty of Montana in motion.

"Undress for me, Martin," she orders him. "I'm always the one who undresses first. Today, I want it to be your turn."

He undresses for her.

Unbuttons the blue shirt and pulls it off. Loosens the belt to his trousers, lowers the zip and lets them fall to the floor. His chest is quite hairy as are his legs, but in a nice way, thinks Montana, not like other men whose body hair is so spidery. The black socks go. He wears old-fashioned low-cut underpants, not the customary boxer shorts. She sees him hold in his stomach as he rolls them down.

His cock is of average length as it stands now, but dark and thick, cut. A forest of black curls spreads across his crotch, a thin tributary line of straighter hairs leads almost all the way up to his navel. His hips are slim, his nipples brown. A dark brown stain, in the shape of some continent, spreads below his left breast to the initial curve of his abdomen, a birthmark he is no longer self-conscious about.

"*Voila!*" he says theatrically. "As nature intended. Not too disappointed I hope? I realise I'm not Adonis."

"Nice," Montana purses her lips and feigns appetite.

He smiles.

"Your turn," he asks gently.

She undresses.

"Oh, Montana!" he says, as she stands nude and, in awe and wonder, moves closer to her.

The bed.

They embrace. Skin to skin. A force field of desire surrounds them, made up of all the lost moments, the craving, the despair and sheer unadulterated lust.

Their hands explore. Horizons of skin to be mapped, sensitivity to be choreographed, intimacies delineated. Sounds of silence. Fingers tiptoe over virgin territory.

Images of love. Of sex.

His hand in her hair, counting every curl like a novice arithmatician.

The moan in her throat when his teeth graze an earlobe.

The fragile nape of her neck.

The muscles rippling calmly in his arms when he holds hers tight.

The precious angle formed by the triangulation of her thighs and pubis.

The muted sound of heartbeats aligning their rhythm.

Mouth touches nipple.

Nipple touches lips.

Lips lick toe.

Toe curls against outer lip.

She parts herself to help his entry.

Her hand strokes his velvet cock, dampens its heat, guides it towards her gaping, humid portals.

"I want you inside me," she shouts. "Now!"

"Yes," he says, in all simplicity.

Connection. Pleasure to the *nth* degree. Their bodies play the two-backed game with utter mechanical precision. He fits inside her like a made-to-measure glove. She is speared, impaled, embedded onto him, knifed by the pulse of his cock moving within, every thrust bringing her one inch nearer to death, to oblivion.

"Deeper" she cries out.

He adjusts his angle of entry by forcing her splayed legs upwards where they rest on his shoulders. Like a a golden drill, he reaches for the walls of her womb, heat against heat, raw tissues scraping against each other in the cavern of obscenity.

The first time is always the best. Tentative, yes. Clumsy, sometimes. But never so full of delicacy and tenderness. Unbelievably, they come together and collapse, short of breath, countless divinities invoked in vain. Silence. They both know that words are now superfluous, that they've crossed their personal Rubicon and moved one step beyond.

But the second time is even better.

Her mouth brings him to hardness again, his lips chew her nipples until the threshold of pain turns into undiluted pleasure. He effortlessly slides two fingers into her rear, turns her over and once again invests her. She is open, a raw, volcanic wound ready to give birth to the scream that is also the name of God. Deeper and deeper he goes inside her. Growing with every successive movement, fertilized by her inner juices. They smell like animals. They are wonderful beasts, rutting, copulating, fucking, without humanity, reduced to the level of brute consciousness. They no longer have names. They are cunt and cock, arse and breasts, mouth and tongue. A new species.

And the third time is pornographically joyful. By now, their bodies reek with familiarity and, as tiredness assails them from all sides, their lust takes complete charge. She rims the circumference of his sphincter, deposits a mouthful of saliva there and slides one finger and then two into him, her nail drawing blood as she digs beneath the surface. His cock surges upwards like the mast of a ship, screaming for release. Her other hand seizes it firmly as she continues to burrow in his most intimate innards, listening both to the pulse of his heart against the blue vein that winds up his erect cock and to the rise within of the volcanic stream he can no longer control. When she senses that his orgasm is about to rush through his mistreated genitals, she quickly positions herself under him and drinks his holy milk as he comes, in thin, exhausted bursts. The sheer contact of her mouth revives his tumescence and she triumphantly spits him out only to rise above his reclining body and straddle him, before lowering herself onto him and sinking her burning cunt on to his trembling pole. The heat within briefly preserves his hardness and as she rides him ferociously, he comes again, his seed like a rocket aimed towards her heart.

Finally, imagination and bodies spent, they sleep. Hand holding hand, spoonlike tight against each other, his shriveled cock against the slight blonde down in the small of her back, her white arse against the top of his thighs, feet and toes intricately knitted together, his breath a murmur against her neck.

Neither wake up until late, both amazed by the sheer intensity of their folly, still awake in the land of their most unlikely dreams. Both feel famished and order breakfast through room service. Then sleep again.

"Is this what we were afraid of, Montana?"

"It is."

"I love you. For real now. I just don't want you to go. Can't bear the thought of you returning to your husband."

"And you to your wife."

"I just wasn't ready for this. Even in my wildest imaginings I never dreamt it could be so strong. Sounds melodramatic, I know, but we were made for each other."

"And that is exactly what I feared, Martin."

"Jesus!"

"That's what I usually say when I come," she smiled.

He smiled back at her.

"I love you, Montana. The feel of your skin, the green lakes of your eyes, the way that you talk, the movement of your hair when you shake your head, the feeling when I am inside you of finally being home."

"And I love your kindness, Martin. From the first time we

spoke online, it felt predestined. I could sense all the things in you that could make me happy, provide me with such incomparable pleasure. It was scary. That's why I initially drew back. Self-preservation. I'm not sure whether I can give myself fully to you as you'd wish."

"I remember an early conversation, Montana. We were talking about love. As always. And you confessed that you had a cold heart. You were so wrong."

"Don't be so sure."

A day and another night. Thirty-six hours in a hotel room, cut off from the outside world.

Sex again and again.

Endless conversations.

Martin asked, begged, implored. They would be together, he could see no other way. He would leave his family, though it would be messy. Money and lawyers would ensure she kept Vanessa, and he and Montana would raise her as if it were his own daughter.

It was now or never.

A chance like this would not repeat itself in their lifetime. It should not be wasted. Happiness was there to be seized, miles and miles of it.

Montana cried. He did likewise.

He cried because of the new life that beckoned. Montana cried because she had never met a man so full of tenderness and quiet poetry. She had known too many other types of men.

Finally, she relented and agreed that they had to go through with it. Run off together. The pieces they could pick up later. Yes, there was no other way.

Plans were made.

But she would need her passport, some clothes.

A parting kiss that would linger for hours in their memory, an embrace, the look of love in her sad eyes.

He would begin making the necessary arrangements and

come and fetch her by taxi mid-afternoon at her house. She would be ready, packed, letter of explanation to husband written begging forgiveness. Martin had suggested that they go first to New York.

"OK, I have to go now," Montana said, "I'll see you this afternoon, then. Don't be late." She wanted them to be out of town by the time her husband returned home and found her note.

"Come on, one last kiss."

"I don't like goodbyes."

He escorted her to the hotel hallway.

"That's it. No further," Montana said.

"I love you . . . Four o'clock?"

"Four o'clock," she answered and made her way through the Royal York's foyer, refusing to look back, a profound sense of emptiness gradually taking hold of what was now left of her heart.

She caught a cab outside the hotel and asked him to circle the block twice before depositing her at the train station's side entrance, which could not be seen from the Royal York windows. The next train to Montreal was leaving ten minutes later. She caught it.

As the express train raced through the northern forests, Montana sat by the window, watching the lush landscape unfurl like a picture postcard brought to life. Her mind was blank, her feelings dead. If she remained on this train, and did not bother to get off in Montreal, she could end up in Calgary or even Vancouver. Just a step from there to Alaska, say. But the cold regions surrounding her heart pined for warmer places really, exotic islands, balmy beaches where she could walk nude and sleep like an innocent, her dreams no longer burdened by all the mistakes and decisions that now littered her past.

The somnambulistic tick-tock of the wheels on the track soon took hold of her and she drifted off to sleep.

❐

Martin was worried that Montana would be angry. He hadn't been able to book them on a flight later today to New York, so had to settle for Boston. The only alternative would have been an Amtrak coach to the Port Ferry Authority off 42nd Street which would have taken an eternity to reach New York. He knew she would be disappointed. She had told him that she had never been to New York and he was so eager to help her discover the city he enjoyed so much. Hopefully once in Boston, he'd be able to get matters back on course and reach Manhattan by the weekend.

His taxi had left the city center and reached the prosperous inner suburbs. They were driving down a pleasant tree-lined street full of fashionable-looking stores. The car drew up to the kerb.

"Are we here?"

"Yes, sir."

As the cab departed, Martin looked at the piece of paper on which he had jotted down Montana's address and checked the number on Bayview Avenue. It corresponded to a bookshop and there did not appear to be any apartments above it. Anyway, she had said she lived in a house often enough. His heart skipped a beat. Maybe the cab driver had made a mistake, misheard him and this was not Bayview Avenue. He hurried to the nearby intersection a hundred yards away to check on the road sign. A hollow pit began forming in his stomach. This was indeed Bayview Avenue.

He rushed into the bookstore. Inquired about Montana Chamaillàrd. Hoping against hope.

No, the name was unknown. Nobody lived there.

He asked the bookseller, a slim dark man stroking a cat as he sat by his cash register, whether he knew of another Bayview Avenue in Toronto. Apparently not. The bookshop had been here nearly ten years and he would have known of another street with the same name. Martin made a further request, cold sweat fast breaking out all over him. The trader obliged by fishing out a telephone book, in which Martin raced to the letter C. There were so many Chamaillards. Seemingly a common name among French Canadians. Several under *M*, but then he realized Montana had never actually disclosed her husband's first name. Martin thanked the bookseller and walked out onto the street. The sun was high but fading behind a cluster of clouds.

She closed the front door softly and, through familiar darkness, made her way to their bedroom, a route she could follow with her eyes closed. She looked into the child's room as she passed it, but all was quiet.

She undressed by the pale light from the window, a quarter moon and distant car lights fading into the distance on the Ontario highway. In the large bed, small Vanessa lie sound asleep in the arms of her father.

Montana smiled weakly and slipped under the covers, feeling their combined warmth reach her as she lay down. Her husband stirred, looked over.

She saw him open his eyes.

"I'm back," she said softly.

He acknowledged her with a sad smile and closed his eyes again. She extended her hand and touched her daughter's skin. She was so soft. The child coughed in her sleep.

The next day, she disconnected her modem from the computer. The "new messages" icon was frantically flashing away. She knew it would be Martin. No doubt in a state of panic, still days from understanding. Did she in fact even understand the whole thing herself? This love thing that just pursued her?

They all pretended everything was normal, as if she had never been away as she laid out the breakfast table with the usual placings and items. There was a broad smile on her daughter's beaming face, and her morning cuddle seemed tighter and longer than before. Her husband kissed her kindly on the cheek after she emerged from the shower, at his usual shaving post.

"Nice to have you back," he said.

"Thank you," Montana said formally, brushing away a speck of shaving cream from her cheek where his lathered upper lip had deposited it. Another old, comforting routine.

After the childminder had come to fetch Vanessa to take her to the nursery school, they both dressed and exchanged small talk. When they would finally go to the local multiplex to catch that Hollywood blockbuster they were both keen to see. About the friends who were coming for a dinner party on Saturday night and what she should cook for them. Talk about servicing his car, which would necessitate him using hers for the day as he couldn't do without wheels for work, and whether those strange vibrations under the hood actually emanated from the engine or just a loose part.

"See you tonight," her husband said as they separated in the street below.

"I do love you," Montana whispered as he moved away. But she wasn't sure he heard her across the noise of the building rush hour traffic to the city.

Six weeks later, Montana discovered she was pregnant. Remembered she had skipped taking the pill for a few days around Toronto time. Her mind so aflutter with other things.

"It's just wonderful," her husband said. "You don't know how happy this news makes me. It's fantastic. Oh, Adrienne!"

He took her in his arms and was close to tears. He had never raised the matter of her sudden absence. Denial or discretion on his part, she wasn't sure.

"Yes," she said. "We're turning a new page."

She knew the child was Martin's. She also knew it would be a boy this time.

Three in the morning. Heart of the night. Montana woke up,

her head so full of future dreams, stirrings of all kinds dancing a salsa in her head. But she felt at peace with herself at last.

She couldn't get back to sleep and moved silently to the study. Thought of the last year. Her mad twelve months. The state of her. The faceless encounters in the airport hotel bars. New York. The bodiless voices of the Internet calling out to her. The painstaking hours in the brownstone typing her daily account of the crazy events she had been part of, while the heartbreaking imprint of the sex was still handwritten deep into every cell of her body.

She switched on the computer, clicked on applications and selected a word processing program.

Stared at the flickering blue screen.

A silent, small epiphany rose inside her, its invisible movements in unison with the seeds of the new life stirring inside her womb. Or was that just her imagination?

Her untamed curls were falling against her eyes.

She threw her hair back. She would have to shorten it one of these days. Maybe get a new look altogether?

And she began typing:

Ohio had never been to Ohio, she writes.

At first, she is hesitant. The lines come slowly. The white screen is a challenge. But, somehow, the words make their way through amongst the anguish. As they always do.

London, Maldives.
Spring, Summer 1998

My Secret Life
Anonymous

Over two million copies sold!

Perhaps the most infamous of all underground Victorian erotica, *My Secret Life* is the sexual memoir of a well-to-do gentleman, who began at an early age to keep a diary of his erotic behavior. He continues this record for over forty years, creating in the process a unique social and psychological document. Its complete and detailed description of the hidden side of British and European life in the nineteenth century furnishes materials for the understanding of the Victorian Age that cannot be duplicated in any other source.

The Altar of Venus
Anonymous

Our author, a gentleman of wealth and privilege, is introduced to desire's delights at a tender age, and then and there commits himself to a life-long sensual expedition. As he enters manhood, he progresses from schoolgirls' charms to older women's enticements, especially those of acquaintances' mothers and wives. Later, he moves beyond common London brothels to sophisticated entertainments available only in Paris. Truly, he has become a lord among libertines.

Caning Able
Stan Kent

Caning Able is a modern-day version of the melodramatic tales of Victorian erotica. Full of dastardly villains, regimented discipline, corporal punishment and forbidden sexual liaisons, the novel features the brilliant and beautiful Jasmine, a seemingly helpless heroine who reigns triumphant despite dire peril. By mixing libidinous prose with a changing business world, *Caning Able* gives treasured plots a welcome twist: women who are definitely not the weaker sex.

The Blue Moon Erotic Reader IV

A testimonial to the publication of quality erotica, *The Blue Moon Erotic Reader IV* presents more than twenty romantic and exciting excerpts from selections spanning a variety of periods and themes. This is a historical compilation that combines generous extracts from the finest forbidden books with the most extravagant samplings that the modern erotica imagination has created. The result is a collection that is provocative, entertaining, and perhaps even enlightening. It encompasses memorable scenes of youthful initiations into the mysteries of sex, notorious confessions, and scandalous adventures of the powerful, wealthy, and notable. From the classic erotica of *Wanton Women*, and *The Intimate Memoirs of an Edwardian Dandy* to modern tales like Michael Hemmingson's *The Rooms*, good taste, passion, and an exalted desire are abound, making for a union of sex and sensibility that is available only once in a Blue Moon.

With selections by Don Winslow, Ray Gordon, M. S. Valentine, P. N. Dedeaux, Rupert Mountjoy, Eve Howard, Lisabet Sarai, Michael Hemmingson, and many others.

The Best of the Erotic Reader

"The Erotic Reader series offers an unequaled selection of the hottest scenes drawn from the finest erotic writing." — *Elle*

This historical compilation contains generous extracts from the world's finest forbidden books including excerpts from *Memories of a Young Don Juan*, *My Secret Life*, *Autobiography of a Flea*, *The Romance of Lust*, *The Three Chums*, and many others. They are gathered together here to entertain, and perhaps even enlighten. From secret texts to the scandalous adventures of famous people, from youthful initiations into the mysteries of sex to the most notorious of all confessions, *Best of the Erotic Reader* is a stirring complement to the senses. Containing the most evocative pieces covering several eras of erotic fiction, *Best of the Erotic Reader* collects the most scintillating tales from the seven volumes of *The Erotic Reader*. This comprehensive volume is sure to include delights for any taste and guaranteed to titillate, amuse, and arouse the interests of even the most veteran erotica reader.

Confessions D'Amour
Anne-Marie Villefranche

Confessions D'Amour is the culmination of Villefranche's comically indecent stories about her friends in 1920s' Paris.

Anne-Marie Villefranche invites you to enter an intoxicating world where men and women arrange their love affairs with skill and style. This is a world where illicit encounters are as smooth as a silk stocking, and where sexual secrets are kept in confidence only until a betrayal can be turned to advantage. Here we follow the adventures of Gabrielle de Michoux, the beautiful young widow who contrives to be maintained in luxury by a succession of well-to-do men, Marcel Chalon, ready for any adventure so long as he can go home to Mama afterwards, Armand Budin, who plunges into a passionate love affair with his cousin's estranged wife, Madelein Beauvais, and Yvonne Hiver who is married with two children while still embracing other, younger lovers.

"An erotic tribute to the Paris of yesteryear that will delight modern readers."—*The Observer*

———

A Maid For All Seasons I, II – Devlin O'Neill

Two Delightful Tales of Romance and Discipline

Lisa is used to her father's old-fashioned discipline, but is it fair that her new employer acts the same way? Mr. Swayne is very handsome, very British and very particular about his new maid's work habits. But isn't nineteen a bit old to be corrected that way? Still, it's quite a different sensation for Lisa when Mr. Swayne shows his displeasure with her behavior. But Mr. Swayne isn't the only man who likes to turn Lisa over his knee. When she goes to college she finds a new mentor, whose expectations of her are even higher than Mr. Swayne's, and who employs very old-fashioned methods to correct Lisa's bad behavior. Whether in a woodshed in Georgia, or a private club in Chicago, there is always someone there willing and eager to take Lisa in hand and show her the error of her ways.

Color of Pain, Shade of Pleasure
Edited by Cecilia Tan

In these twenty-one tales from two out-of-print classics, *Fetish Fantastic* and *S/M Futures*, some of today's most unflinching erotic fantasists turn their futuristic visions to the extreme underground, transforming the modern fetishes of S/M, bondage, and eroticized power exchange into the templates for new sexual worlds. From the near future of S/M in cyberspace, to a future police state where the real power lies in manipulating authority, these tales are from the edge of both sexual and science fiction.

The Governess
M. S. Valentine

Lovely Miss Hunnicut eagerly embarks upon a career as a governess, hoping to escape the memories of her broken engagement. Little does she know that Crawleigh Manor is far from the respectable household it appears to be. Mr. Crawleigh, in particular, devotes himself to Miss Hunnicut's thorough defiling. Soon the young governess proves herself worthy of the perverse master of the house—though there may be even more depraved powers at work in gloomy Crawleigh Manor . . .

Claire's Uptown Girls
Don Winslow

In this revised and expanded edition, Don Winslow introduces us to Claire's girls, the most exclusive and glamorous escorts in the world. Solicited by upper-class Park Avenue businessmen, Claire's girls have the style, glamour and beauty to charm any man. Graced with super-model beauty, a meticulously crafted look, and a willingness to fulfill any man's most intimate dream, these girls are sure to fulfill any man's most lavish and extravagant fantasy.

The Intimate Memoirs of an Edwardian Dandy I, II, III
Anonymous

This is the sexual coming-of-age of a young Englishman from his youthful days on the countryside to his educational days at Oxford and finally as a sexually adventurous young man in the wild streets of London. Having the free time and money that comes with a privileged upbringing, coupled with a free spirit, our hero indulges every one of his, and our, sexual fantasies. From exotic orgies with country maidens to fanciful escapades with the London elite, the young rake experiences it all. A lusty tale of sexual adventure, *The Intimate Memoirs of an Edwardian Dandy* is a celebration of free spirit and experimentation.

"A treat for the connoisseur of erotic literature."
—*The Guardian*

Jennifer and Nikki
D. M. Perkins

From Manhattan's Fifth Avenue, to the lush island of Tobago, to a mysterious ashram in upstate New York, Jennifer travels with reclusive fashion model Nikki and her seductive half-brother Alain in search of the sexual secrets held by the famous Russian mystic Pere Mitya. To achieve intimacy with this extraordinary family, and get the story she has promised to Jack August, dynamic publisher of *New Man Magazine,* Jennifer must ignore universal taboos and strip away inhibitions she never knew she had.

Confessions of a Left Bank Dominatrix
Gala Fur

Gala Fur introduces the world of French S&M with two collections of stories in one delectable volume. In *Souvenirs of a Left Bank Dominatrix*, stories address topics as varied as: how to recruit a male maidservant, how to turn your partner into a marionette, and how to use a cell phone to humiliate a submissive in a crowded train station. In *Sessions*, Gala offers more description of the life of a dominatrix, detailing the marathon of "Lesbians, bisexuals, submissivies, masochists, paying customers [and] passing playmates" that seek her out for her unique sexual services.

"An intoxicating sexual romp." —*Evergreen Review*

Don Winslow's Victorian Erotica
Don Winslow

The English manor house has long been a place apart; a place of elegant living where, in splendid isolation the gentry could freely indulge their passions for the outdoor sports of riding and hunting. Of course, there were those whose passions ran towards "indoor sports"—lascivious activities enthusiastically, if discreetly, pursued by lusty men and sensual women behind large and imposing stone walls of baronial splendor, where they were safely hidden from prying eyes. These are tales of such licentious decadence from behind the walls of those stately houses of a bygone era.

The Garden of Love
Michael Hemmingson

Three Erotic Thrillers from the Master of the Genre

In The *Comfort of Women*, the oddly passive Nicky Bayless undergoes a sexual re-education at the hands (and not only the hands) of a parade of desperate women who both lead and follow him through an underworld of erotic extremity. The narrator of *The Dress* is troubled by a simple object that may have supernatural properties. "My wife changed when she wore The Dress; she was the Ashley who came to being a few months ago. She was the wife I preferred, and I worried about that. I understood that The Dress was, indeed, an entity all its own, with its own agenda, and it was possessing my wife." In *Drama*, playwright Jonathan falls into an affair with actress Karen after the collapse of his relationship with director Kristine. But Karen's free-fall into debauchery threatens to destroy them both.

The ABZ of Pain and Pleasure
Edited by A. M. LeDeluge

A true alphabet of the unusual, *The ABZ of Pain and Pleasure* offers the reader an understanding of the language of the lash. Beginning with Aida and culminating with Zanetti, this book offers the amateur and adept a broad acquaintance with the heroes and heroines of this unique form of sexual entertainment. The Marquis de Sade is represented here, as are Jean de Berg (author of *The Image*), Pauline Réage (author of *The Story of O* and *Return to the Château*), P. N. Dedeaux (author of *The Tutor* and *The Prefect*), and twenty-two others.

"Frank" and I
Anonymous

The narrator of the story, a wealthy young man, meets a youth one day—the "Frank" of the title—and, taken by his beauty and good manners, invites him to come home with him. One can only imagine his surprise when the young man turns out to be a young woman with beguiling charms.

Hot Sheets
Ray Gordon

Running his own hotel, Mike Hunt struggles to make ends meet. In an attempt to attract more patrons, he turns Room 69 into a state-of-the-art sex chamber. Now all he has to do is wait and watch the money roll in. But nympho waitresses, a sex-crazed chef, and a bartender obsessed with adult videos don't exactly make the ideal hotel staff. And big trouble awaits Mike when his enterprise is infiltrated by an attractive undercover policewoman.

Tea and Spices
Nina Roy

Revolt is seething in the loins of the British colonial settlement of Uttar Pradesh, and in the heart of memsahib Devora Hawthorne who lusts after the dark, sultry Rohan, her husband's trusted servant. While Rohan educates Devora in the intricate social codes that govern the mean-spirited colonial community, he also introduces his eager mistress to a way of loving that exceeds the English imagination. Together, the two explore sexual territories that neither class nor color can control.

Naughty Message
Stanley Carten

Wesley Arthur is a withdrawn computer engineer who finds little excitement in his day-to-day life. That is until the day he comes home from work to discover a lascivious message on his answering machine. Aroused beyond his wildest dreams by the unmentionable acts described, Wesley becomes obsessed with tracking down the woman behind the seductive and mysterious voice. His search takes him through phone sex services, strip clubs and no-tell motels—and finally to his randy reward . . .

The Sleeping Palace
M. Orlando

Another thrilling volume of erotic reveries from the author of *The Architecture of Desire*. Maison Bizarre is the scene of unspeakable erotic cruelty; the Lust Akademie holds captive only the most debauched students of the sensual arts; Baden-Eros is the luxurious retreat of one's most prurient dreams. Once again, M. Orlando uses his flair for exotic detail to explore the nether regions of desire.

"Orlando's writing is an orgasmic and linguistic treat." —*Skin Two*

Venus in Paris
Florentine Vaudrez

When a woman discovers the depths of her own erotic nature, her enthusiasm for the games of love become a threat to her husband. Her older sister defies the conventions of Parisian society by living openly with her lover, a man destined to deceive her. Together, these beautiful sisters tread the path of erotic delight—first in the arms of men, and then in the embraces of their own, more subtle and more constant sex.

The Lawyer
Michael Hemmingson

Drama tells the titillating story of bad karma and kinky sex among the thespians of The Alfred Jarry Theater.

In this erotic legal thriller, Michael Hemmingson explores sexual perversity within the judicial system. Kelly O'Rourke is an editorial assistant at a large publishing house—she has filed a lawsuit against the conglomerate's best-selling author after a questionable night on a yacht. Kelly isn't quite as innocent as she seems, rather, as her lawyer soon finds out, she has a sordid history of sexual deviance and BDSM, which may not be completely in her past.

Tropic of Lust
Michele de Saint-Exupery

She was the beautiful young wife of a respectable diplomat posted to Bangkok. There the permissive climate encouraged even the most outré sexual fantasy to become reality. Anything was possible for a woman ready to open herself to sexual discovery.

"A tale of sophisticated sensuality [it is] the story of a woman who dares to explore the depths of her own erotic nature."—*Avant Garde*

Folies D'Amour
Anne-Marie Villefranche

From the international best-selling pen of Anne-Marie Villefranche comes another 'improper' novel about the affairs of an intimate circle of friends and lovers. In the stylish Paris of the 1920s, games of love are played with reckless abandon. From the back streets of Montmartre to the opulent hotels on the Rue de Rivoli, the City of Light casts an erotic spell.

The Best of Ironwood
Don Winslow

Ostensibly a finishing school for young ladies, Ironwood is actually that singular institution where submissive young beauties are rigorously trained in the many arts of love. For James, our young narrator, Ironwood is a world where discipline knows few boundaries. This collection gathers the very best selections from the Ironwood series and reveals the essence of the Ironwood woman—a consummate blend of sexuality and innocence.

The Uninhibited
Ray Gordon

Donna Ryan works in a research laboratory where her boss has developed a new hormone treatment with some astounding and unsuspected side effects. Any woman who comes into contact with the treatment finds her sexual urges so dramatically increased that she loses all her inhibitions. Donna accidentally picks up one of the patches and finds her previously suppressed cravings erupting in an ecstatic orgy of liberated impulses. What ensues is a breakthrough to thrilling dimensions of wild, unrestrained sexuality.

Blue Angel Nights
Margarete von Falkensee

This is the delightfully wicked story of an era of infinite possibilities—especially when it comes to eroticism in all its bewitching forms. Among actors and aristocrats, with students and showgirls, in the cafes and salons, and at backstage parties in pleasure boudoirs, *Blue Angel Nights* describes the time when even the most outlandish proposal is likely to find an eager accomplice.

Disciplining Jane
by Jane Eyre

Retaining the threatening and sadistic intent of Charlotte Bronte's *Jane Eyre*, *Disciplining Jane* retells the story with an erotic twist. After enduring constant scrutiny from her cruel adoptive family, young Jane is sent to Lowood, a boarding school where Jane is taught the ways of the rod that render her first in her class.

———

66 Chapters About 33 Women
Michael Hemmingson

An erotic tour de force, *66 Chapters About 33 Women* weaves a complicated web of erotic connections between 33 women and their lovers. Granting each woman 2 vignettes, Hemmingson examines their sexual peccadilloes, and creates a veritable survey course on the possibilities of erotic fiction.

———

The Man of Her Dream
Briony Shilton

Spun from her subconscious's submissive nature, a woman dreams of a man like no other, one who will subject her to pain and pressure, passion and lust. She searches the waking world, combing her personal history and exploring fantasy and fact, until she finds this master. It is he, through an initiation like no other, who takes her to the limits of her submissive nature and on to the extremes of pure sexual joy.

———

S-M: The Last Taboo
Gerald and Caroline Greene

A unique effort to abolish the negative stereotypes that have permeated our perception of sadomasochism. *S-M* illuminates the controversy over the practice as a whole and its place in our culture. The book addresses such topics as: the role of women in sadomasochism; American society and Masochism; the true nature of the Marquis de Sade; spanking in various countries; undinism, more popularly known as "water sports"; and general s-m scenarios. Accompanying the text is a complete appendix of s-m documents, ranging from the steamy works of Baudelaire to Pauline Reage's *Story of O*.

Cybersex
Miranda Reigns

Collected for the first time in one volume is the entirety of Miranda Reigns's *Cyberwebs* trilogy. The trilogy follows Miranda, a young woman who indulges her darkest fantasies by plunging deep into the depths of the online erotic community. But, she soon finds that she cannot separate her online life from her real relationships. Riddled with guilt, Miranda attempts to untangle herself from these relationships, but finds that in the battle between morality and passion, it is the lascivious side of her that always wins.

Depravicus
Anonymous

The Reverend William Entercock is the highly unorthodox priest of Cumsdale Church. As well as running various lucrative undercover commercial enterprises the randy rev also enjoys distinctly worldly relationships with a range of the parish's young ladies, including the nuns. Bishop Simon Holesgood has his suspicions about the vivacious vicar. Joined by a vengeful Mother Superior, the Bishop sets out to get Entercock defrocked. Worse, an attractive young tabloid journalist wants to expose him for the sake of the sensational story that revelation of his excesses will make.

Sacred Exchange
Edited by Lisabet Sarai and S. F. Mayfair

Sacred Exchange is an anthology of original erotic fiction that explores the transcendent, spiritual, or magical aspects of the power exchange in Dominance and Submission. Through stories of ritual, communion, telepathy, devotion, dreams, commitment, and intense personal change, *Sacred Exchange* examines how the bond of trust between dominant and submissive can lead to emotional and spiritual revelations.

The Rooms
Michael Hemmingson

Danielle is the ultimate submissive, begging to do the nastiest, kinkiest acts for a Master. Two men, Alex and Gordon, have sexually enslaved her. They also happen to be her college professors. She opens the darkest regions of her slutty soul to them, revealing rooms of sexual adventure they never knew existed.

The Memoirs of Josephine
Anonymous

19th Century Vienna was a wellspring of culture, society and decadence and home to Josephine Mutzenbacher. One of the most beautiful and sought after libertines of the age, she rose from the streets to become a celebrated courtesan. As a young girl, she learned the secrets of her profession. As mistress to wealthy, powerful men, she used her talents to transform from a slattern to the most wanted woman of the age. This candid, long suppressed memoir is her story.

The Pearl
Anonymous

Lewd, bawdy, and sensual, this cult classic is a collection of Victorian erotica that circulated in an underground magazine known as *The Pearl* from July 1879 to December 1880. Now dusted off and totally uncensored, the journal of voluptuous reading that titillated the eminent Victorians is reprinted in its entirety. The eighteen issues of *The Pearl* are packed with short stories, naughty poems, ballads of sexual adventure, letters, limericks, jokes, gossip, and six serialized novels.

Mistress of Instruction
Christine Kerr

Mistress of Instruction is a delightfully erotic romp through merry old Victorian England. Gillian, precocious and promiscuous, travels to London where she discovers Crawford House, an exclusive gentlemen's club where young ladies are trained to excel in service. A true prodigy of sensual talents, she is retained to supervise the other girls' initiation into "the life." Her title: Mistress of Instruction.

Neptune and Surf
Marilyn Jaye Lewis

A trio of lyrical yet explicit novellas sure to challenge stereotypes about the stylistic range of women's erotica. *Neptune and Surf* is the fruit of the author's conversations with a group of women about their deepest fantasies. What arises is a tantalizing look at women's libidinous desires, exploring their deepest fantasies with a mesmerizing delicacy and frankness. With *Neptune and Surf* Lewis shows why she is one of the premier female voices in erotica.

Order These Selected Blue Moon Titles

My Secret Life $15.95
The Altar of Venus.....................$7.95
Caning Able $7.95
The Blue Moon Erotic Reader IV $15.95
The Best of the Erotic Reader...........$15.95
Confessions D'Amour $14.95
A Maid for All Seasons I, II $15.95
Color of Pain, Shade of Pleasure $14.95
The Governess $7.95
Claire's Uptown Girls $7.95
The Intimate Memoirs of an
Edwardian Dandy I, II, III............. $15.95
Jennifer and Nikki $7.95
Burn $7.95
Don Winslow's Victorian Erotica $14.95
The Garden of Love $14.95
The ABZ of Pain and Pleasure $7.95
"Frank" and I..........................$7.95
Hot Sheets $7.95
Tea and Spices $7.95
Naughty Message $7.95
The Sleeping Palace....................$7.95
Venus in Paris $7.95
The Lawyer $7.95
Tropic of Lust $7.95
Folies D'Amour $7.95
The Best of Ironwood $14.95

The Uninhibited $7.95
Disciplining Jane $7.95
66 Chapters About 33 Women $7.95
The Man of Her Dream $7.95
S-M: The Last Taboo...................$14.95
Cybersex $14.95
Depravicus $7.95
Sacred Exchange $14.95
The Rooms............................$7.95
The Memoirs of Josephine $7.95
The Pearl $14.95
Mistress of Instruction $7.95
Neptune and Surf $7.95
House of Dreams: Aurochs & Angels ...$7.95
Dark Star..............................$7.95
The Intimate Memoir of Dame Jenny Everleigh:
Erotic Adventures $7.95
Shadow Lane VI $7.95
Shadow Lane VII $7.95
Shadow Lane VIII $7.95
Best of Shadow Lane $14.95
The Captive I, II $14.95
The Captive III, IV, V $15.95
The Captive's Journey $7.95
Road Babe $7.95
The Story of O $7.95
The New Story of O $7.95

ORDER FORM
Attach a separate sheet for additional titles.

Title   Quantity   Price

_____   _____   _____

_____   _____   _____

_____   _____   _____

_____   _____   _____

Shipping and Handling (see charges below)   _____

Sales tax (in CA and NY)   _____

Total   _____

Name _____

Address _____

City _____ State _____ Zip _____

Daytime telephone number _____

❏ Check   ❏ Money Order   (US dollars only. No COD orders accepted.)

Credit Card # _____ Exp. Date _____

❏ MC   ❏ VISA   ❏ AMEX

Signature _____

(if paying with a credit card you must sign this form.)

Shipping and Handling charges:*

Domestic: $4 for 1st book, $.75 each additional book. International: $5 for 1st book, $1 each additional book
*rates in effect at time of publication. Subject to Change.

Mail order to Publishers Group West, Attention: Order Dept., 1700 Fourth St., Berkeley, CA 94710, or fax to (510) 528-3444.

PLEASE ALLOW 4-6 WEEKS FOR DELIVERY. ALL ORDERS SHIP VIA 4TH CLASS MAIL.

Look for Blue Moon Books at your favorite local bookseller or from your favorite online bookseller.